A Boy's Town

by William Dean Howells

I.

EARLIEST EXPERIENCES.

I call it a Boy's Town because I wish it to appear to the reader as a town appears to a boy from his third to his eleventh year, when he seldom, if ever, catches a glimpse of life much higher than the middle of a man, and has the most distorted and mistaken views of most things. He may then indeed look up to the sky, and see heaven open, and angels ascending and descending; but he can only grope about on the earth, and he knows nothing aright that goes on there beyond his small boy's world. Some people remain in this condition as long as they live, and keep the ignorance of childhood, after they have lost its innocence; heaven has been shut, but the earth is still a prison to them. These will not know what I mean by much that I shall have to say; but I hope that the ungrown-up children will, and that the boys who read *Harper's Young People* will like to know what a boy of forty years ago was like, even if he had no very exciting adventures or thread-bare escapes; perhaps I mean hair-breadth escapes; but it is the same thing—they have been used so often. I shall try to describe him very minutely in his daily doings and dreamings, and it may amuse them to compare these doings and dreamings with their own. For convenience, I shall call this boy, my boy; but I hope he might have been almost anybody's boy; and I mean him sometimes for a boy in general, as well as a boy in particular.

THE "FIRST LOCK."

It seems to me that my Boy's Town was a town peculiarly adapted for a boy to be a boy in. It had a river, the great Miami River, which was as blue as the sky when it was not as yellow as gold; and it had another river, called the Old River, which was the Miami's former channel, and which held an island in its sluggish loop; the boys called it The Island; and it must have been about the size of Australia; perhaps it was not so large. Then this town had a Canal, and a Canal-Basin, and a First Lock and a Second Lock; you could walk out to the First Lock, but the Second Lock was at the edge of the known world, and, when my boy was very little, the biggest boy had never been beyond it. Then it had a Hydraulic, which brought the waters of Old River for mill power through the heart of the town, from a Big Reservoir and a Little Reservoir; the Big Reservoir was as far off as the Second Lock, and the Hydraulic ran under mysterious culverts at every street-crossing. All these streams and courses had fish in them at all seasons, and all summer long they had boys in them, and now and then a boy in winter, when the thin ice of the mild Southern Ohio winter let him through with his skates. Then there were the Commons; a wide expanse of open fields, where the cows were pastured, and the boys flew their kites, and ran races, and practised for their circuses in the tan-bark rings of the real circuses.

There were flocks of wild ducks on the Reservoirs and on Old River, and flocks of kildees on the Commons; and there were squirrels in the woods, where there was abundant mast for the pigs that ran wild in them, and battened on the nuts under the hickory-trees. There were no other nuts except walnuts, white and black; but there was no end to the small, sweetish acorns, which the boys called chinquepins; they ate them, but I doubt if they liked them, except as boys like anything to eat. In the vast corn-fields stretching everywhere along the river levels there were quails; and rabbits in the sumac thickets and turnip patches. There were places to swim, to fish, to hunt, to skate; if there were no hills for coasting, that was not so much loss, for there was very little snow, and it melted in a day or two after it fell. But besides these natural advantages for boys, there were artificial opportunities which the boys treated as if they had been made for them; grist-mills on the river and canal, cotton-factories and saw-mills on the Hydraulic, iron-founderies by the Commons, breweries on the river-bank, and not too many school-houses. I must not forget the market-house, with its public market twice a week, and its long rows of market-wagons, stretching on either side of High Street in the dim light of the summer dawn or the cold sun of the winter noon.

The place had its brief history running back to the beginning of the century. Mad Anthony Wayne encamped on its site when he went north to avenge St. Clair's defeat on the Indians; it was at first a fort, and it remained a military post until the tribes about were reduced, and a fort was no longer needed. To this time belonged a tragedy, which my boy knew of vaguely when he was a child. Two of the soldiers were sentenced to be hanged for desertion, and the officer in command hurried forward the execution, although an express had been sent to lay the case before the general at another post. The offence was only a desertion in name, and the reprieve was promptly granted, but it came fifteen minutes too late.

I believe nothing more memorable ever happened in my Boy's Town, as the grown-up world counts events; but for the boys there, every day was full of wonderful occurrence and thrilling excitement. It was really a very simple little town of some three thousand people, living for the most part in small one-story wooden houses, with here and there a brick house of two stories, and here and there a lingering log-cabin, when my boy's father came to take charge of its Whig newspaper in 1840. It stretched eastward from the river to the Canal-Basin, with the market-house, the county buildings, and the stores and hotels on one street, and a few other stores and taverns scattering off on streets that branched from it to the southward; but all this was a vast metropolis to my boy's fancy, where he might get lost—the sum of all disaster—if he ventured away from the neighborhood of the house where he first lived, on its southwestern border. It was the great political year of "Tippecanoe and Tyler too," when the grandfather of our President Harrison was elected President; but the wild hard-cider campaign roared by my boy's little life without leaving a trace in it, except the recollection of his father wearing a linsey-woolsey hunting-shirt, belted at the waist and fringed at the skirt, as a Whig who loved his cause and honored the good old pioneer times was bound to do. I dare say he did not wear it often, and I fancy he wore it then in rather an ironical spirit, for he was a man who had slight esteem for outward shows and semblances; but it remained in my boy's mind, as clear a vision as the long cloak of blue broadcloth in which he must have seen his father habitually. This cloak was such a garment as people still drape about them in Italy, and men wore it in America then instead of an overcoat. To get under its border, and hold by his father's hand in the warmth and dark it made around him was something that the boy thought a great privilege, and that brought him a sense of mystery and security at once that nothing else could ever give. He used to be allowed to go as far as the street corner, to enjoy it, when his father came home from the printing-office in the evening; and one evening, never to be forgotten, after he had long been teasing for a little axe he wanted, he divined that his father had something hidden under his cloak. Perhaps he asked him as usual whether he had brought him the little axe, but his father said, "Feel, feel!" and he found his treasure. He ran home and fell upon the woodpile with it, in a zeal that proposed to leave nothing but chips; before he had gone far he learned that this is a world in which you can sate but never satisfy yourself with anything, even hard work. Some of my readers may have found that out, too; at any rate, my boy did not keep the family in firewood with his axe, and his abiding association with it in after-life was a feeling of weariness and disgust; so I fancy that he must have been laughed at for it. Besides the surfeit of this little axe, he could recall, when he grew up, the glory of wearing his Philadelphia suit, which one of his grandmothers had brought him Over the Mountains, as people said in those days, after a visit to her Pennsylvania German kindred beyond the Alleghanies. It was of some beatified plaid in gay colors, and when once it was put on it never was laid aside for any other suit till it was worn out. It testified unmistakably to the boy's advance in years beyond the shameful period of skirts; and no doubt it commended him to the shadowy little girl who lived so far away as to be even beyond the street-corner, and who used to look for him, as he passed, through the palings of a garden among hollyhocks and four-o'clocks.

The Young People may have heard it said that a savage is a grown-up child, but it seems to me even more true that a child is a savage. Like the savage, he dwells on an earth round which the whole solar system revolves, and he is himself the centre of all life on the earth. It has no meaning but as it relates to him; it is for his pleasure, his use; it is for his pain and his abuse. It is full of sights, sounds, sensations, for his delight alone, for his suffering alone. He lives under a law of favor or of fear, but never of justice, and the savage does not make a crueller idol than the child makes of the Power ruling over his world and having him for its chief concern. What remained to my boy of that faint childish consciousness was the idea of some sort of supernal Being who abode in the skies for his advantage and disadvantage, and made winter and summer, wet weather and dry, with an eye single to him; of a family of which he was necessarily the centre, and of that far, vast, unknown Town, lurking all round him, and existing on account of him if not because of him. So, unless I manage to treat my Boy's Town as a part of his own being, I shall not make others know it just as he knew it.

Some of his memories reach a time earlier than his third year, and relate to the little Ohio River hamlet where he was born, and where his mother's people, who were river-faring folk, all lived. Every two or three years the river rose and flooded the village; and his grandmother's household was taken out of the second-story window in a skiff; but no one minded a trivial inconvenience like that, any more than the Romans have minded the annual freshet of the Tiber for the last three or four thousand years. When the waters went down the family returned and scrubbed out the five or six inches of rich mud they had left. In the meantime, it was a godsend to all boys of an age to enjoy it; but it was nothing out of the order of Providence. So, if my boy ever saw a freshet, it naturally made no impression upon him. What he remembered was something much more important, and that was waking up one morning and seeing a peach-tree in bloom through the window beside his bed; and he was always glad that this vision of beauty was his very earliest memory. All his life he has never seen a peach-tree in bloom without a swelling of the heart, without some fleeting sense that

"Heaven lies about us in our infancy."

Over the spot where the little house once stood, a railroad has drawn its erasing lines, and the house itself was long since taken down and built up brick by brick in quite another place; but the blooming peach-tree glows before his childish eyes untouched by time or change. The tender, pathetic pink of its flowers repeated itself many long years afterwards in the paler tints of the almond blossoms in Italy, but always with a reminiscence of that dim past, and the little coal-smoky town on the banks of the Ohio.

"THE PASSENGER IS A ONE-LEGGED MAN."

Perversely blended with that vision of the blooming peach is a glimpse of a pet deer in the kitchen of the same little house, with his head up and his antlers erect, as if he meditated offence. My boy might never have seen him so; he may have had the vision at second hand; but it is certain that there was a pet deer in the family, and that he was as likely to have come into the kitchen by the window as by the door. One of the boy's uncles had seen this deer swimming the Mississippi, far to the southward, and had sent out a yawl and captured him, and brought him home. He began a checkered career of uselessness when they were ferrying him over from Wheeling in a skiff, by trying to help wear the pantaloons of the boy who was holding him; he put one of his fore-legs in at the watch-pocket; but it was disagreeable to the boy and ruinous to the trousers. He grew very tame, and butted children over, right and left, in the village streets; and he behaved like one of the family whenever he got into a house; he ate the sugar out of the bowl on the table, and plundered the pantry of its sweet cakes. One day a dog got after him, and he jumped over the river-bank and broke his leg, and had to be shot.

Besides the peach-tree and the pet deer there was only one other thing that my boy could remember, or seem to remember, of the few years before he came to the Boy's Town. He is on the steamboat which is carrying the family down the Ohio River to Cincinnati, on their way to the Boy's Town, and he is kneeling on the window-seat in the ladies' cabin at the stern of the boat, watching the rain fall into the swirling yellow river and make the little men jump up from the water with its pelting drops. He knows that the boat is standing still, and they are bringing off a passenger to it in a yawl, as they used to do on the Western rivers when they were hailed from some place where there was no wharf-boat. If they were going down stream, they turned the boat and headed up the river, and then with a great deal of scurrying about among the deck-hands, and swearing among the mates, they sent the yawl ashore, and bustled the passenger on board. In the case which my boy seemed to remember, the passenger is a one-legged man, and he is standing in the yawl, with his crutch under his arm, and his cane in his other hand; his family must be watching him from the house. When the yawl comes alongside he tries to step aboard the steamboat, but he misses his footing and slips into the yellow river, and vanishes softly. It is all so smooth and easy, and it is as curious as the little men jumping up from the rain-drops. What made my boy think when he grew a man that this was truly a memory was that he remembered nothing else of the incident, nothing whatever after the man went down in the water, though there must have been a great and painful tumult, and a vain search for him. His drowning had exactly the value in the child's mind that the jumping up of the little men had, neither more nor less.

II.
HOME AND KINDRED.
As the Boy's Town was, in one sense, merely a part of the boy, I think I had better tell something about my boy's family first, and the influences that formed his character, so that the reader can be a boy with him there on the intimate terms which are the only terms of true friendship. His great-grandfather was a prosperous manufacturer of Welsh flannels, who had founded his industry in a pretty town called The Hay, on the river Wye, in South Wales, where the boy saw one of his mills, still making Welsh flannels, when he visited his father's birthplace a few years ago. This great-grandfather was a Friend by Convincement, as the Quakers say; that is, he was a convert, and not a born Friend, and he had the zeal of a convert. He loved equality and fraternity, and he came out to America towards the close of the last century to prospect for these as well as for a good location to manufacture Welsh flannels; but after being presented to Washington, then President, at Philadelphia, and buying a tract of land somewhere near the District of Columbia, his phantom rolls a shadowy barrel of dollars on board ship at Baltimore, and sails back in the *Flying Dutchman* to South Wales. I fancy, from the tradition of the dollars, that he had made good affairs here with the stock of flannels he brought over with him; but all is rather uncertain about him, especially the land he bought, though the story of it is pretty sure to fire some descendant of his in each new generation with the wish to go down to Washington, and oust the people there who have unrightfully squatted on the ancestral property. What is unquestionable is that this old gentleman went home and never came out here again; but his son, who had inherited all his radicalism, sailed with his family for Boston in 1808, when my boy's father was a year old. From Boston he passed to one Quaker neighborhood after another, in New York, Virginia, and Ohio, setting up the machinery of woollen mills, and finally, after much disastrous experiment in farming, paused at the Boy's Town, and established himself in the drug and book business: drugs and books are still sold together, I believe, in small places. He had long ceased to be a Quaker, but he remained a Friend to every righteous cause; and brought shame to his grandson's soul by being an abolitionist in days when it was infamy to wish the slaves set free. My boy's father restored his self-respect in a measure by being a Henry Clay Whig, or a constitutional anti-slavery man. The grandfather was a fervent Methodist, but the father, after many years of scepticism, had become a receiver of the doctrines of Emanuel Swedenborg; and in this faith the children were brought up. It was not only their faith, but their life, and I may say that in this sense they were a very religious household, though they never went to church, because it was the Old Church. They had no service of the New Church, the Swedenborgians were so few in the place,

except when some of its ministers stopped with us on their travels. My boy regarded these good men as all personally sacred, and while one of them was in the house he had some relief from the fear in which his days seem mostly to have been passed; as if he were for the time being under the protection of a spiritual lightning-rod. Their religion was not much understood by their neighbors of the Old Church, who thought them a kind of Universalists. But the boy once heard his father explain to one of them that the New Church people believed in a hell, which each cast himself into if he loved the evil rather than the good, and that no mercy could keep him out of without destroying him, for a man's love was his very self. It made his blood run cold, and he resolved that rather than cast himself into hell, he would do his poor best to love the good. The children were taught when they teased one another that there was nothing the fiends so much delighted in as teasing. When they were angry and revengeful, they were told that now they were calling evil spirits about them, and that the good angels could not come near them if they wished while they were in that state. My boy preferred the company of good angels after dark, and especially about bedtime, and he usually made the effort to get himself into an accessible frame of mind before he slept; by day he felt that he could look out for himself, and gave way to the natural man like other boys. I suppose the children had their unwholesome spiritual pride in being different from their fellows in religion; but, on the other hand, it taught them not to fear being different from others if they believed themselves right. Perhaps it made my boy rather like it.

The grandfather was of a gloomy spirit, but of a tender and loving heart, whose usual word with a child, when he caressed it, was "Poor thing, poor thing!" as if he could only pity it; and I have no doubt the father's religion was a true affliction to him. The children were taken to visit their grandmother every Sunday noon, and then the father and grandfather never failed to have it out about the New Church and the Old. I am afraid that the father would sometimes forget his own precepts, and tease a little; when the mother went with him she was sometimes troubled at the warmth with which the controversy raged. The grandmother seemed to be bored by it, and the boys, who cared nothing for salvation in the abstract, no matter how anxious they were about the main chance, certainly shared this feeling with her. She was a pale, little, large-eyed lady, who always wore a dress of Quakerish plainness, with a white kerchief crossed upon her breast; and her aquiline nose and jutting chin almost met. She was very good to the children and at these times she usually gave them some sugar-cakes, and sent them out in the yard, where there was a young Newfoundland dog, of loose morals and no religious ideas, who joined them in having fun, till the father came out and led them home. He would not have allowed them to play where it could have aggrieved any one, for a prime article of his religion was to respect the religious feelings of others, even when he thought them wrong. But he would not suffer the children to get the notion that they were guilty of any deadly crime if they happened to come short of the conventional standard of piety. Once, when their grandfather reported to him that the boys had been seen throwing stones on Sunday at the body of a dog lodged on some drift in the river, he rebuked them for the indecorum, and then ended the matter, as he often did, by saying, "Boys, consider yourselves soundly thrashed."

I should be sorry if anything I have said should give the idea that their behavior was either fantastic or arrogant through their religion. It was simply a pervading influence; and I am sure that in the father and mother it dignified life, and freighted motive and action here with the significance of eternal fate. When the children were taught that in every thought and in every deed they were choosing their portion with the devils or the angels, and that God himself could not save them against themselves, it often went in and out of their minds, as such things must with children; but some impression remained and helped them to realize the serious responsibility they were under to their own after-selves. At the same time, the father, who loved a joke almost as much as he loved a truth, and who despised austerity as something owlish, set them the example of getting all the harmless fun they could out of experience. They had their laugh about nearly everything that was not essentially sacred; they were made to feel the ludicrous as an alleviation of existence; and the father and mother were with them on the same level in all this enjoyment.

The house was pretty full of children, big and little. There were seven of them in the Boy's Town, and eight afterwards in all; so that if there had been no Boy's Town about them, they would still have had a Boy's World indoors. They lived in three different houses—the Thomas house, the Smith house, and the Falconer house—severally called after the names of their owners, for they never had a house of their own. Of the first my boy remembered nothing, except the woodpile on which he tried his axe, and a closet near the front door, which he entered into one day, with his mother's leave, to pray, as the Scripture bade. It was very dark, and hung full of clothes, and his literal application of the text was not edifying; he fancied, with a child's vague suspicion, that it amused his father and mother; I dare say it also touched them. Of the Smith house, he could remember much more: the little upper room where the boys slept, and the narrow stairs which he often rolled down in the morning; the front room where he lay sick with a fever, and was bled by the doctor, as people used to be in those days; the woodshed where, one dreadful afternoon, when he had somehow been left alone in the house, he took it into his head that the family dog Tip was going mad; the window where he traced the figure of a bull on greased paper from an engraving held up against the light: none of them important facts, but such as stick in the mind by the capricious action of memory, while far greater events drop out of it. My boy's elder brother at once accused him of tracing that bull, which he pretended to have copied; but their father insisted upon taking the child's word for it, though he must have known he was lying; and this gave my boy a far worse conscience than if his father had whipped him. The father's theory was that people are more apt to be true if you trust them than if you doubt them; I do not think he always found it work perfectly; but I believe he was right.

My boy was for a long time very miserable about that bull, and the experience taught him to desire the truth and honor it, even when he could not attain it. Five or six years after, when his brother and he had begun to read stories, they found one in the old *New York Mirror* which had a great influence upon their daily conduct. It was called "The Trippings of Tom Pepper; or, the Effects of Romancing," and it showed how at many important moments the hero had been baulked of fortune by his habit of fibbing. They took counsel together, and pledged themselves not to tell the smallest lie, upon any occasion whatever. It was a frightful slavery, for there are a great many times in a boy's life when it seems as if the truth really could not serve him. Their great trial was having to take a younger brother with them whenever they wanted to go off with other boys; and it had been their habit to get away from him by many little deceits which they could not practise now: to tell him that their mother wanted him; or to send him home upon some errand to his pretended advantage that had really no object but his absence. I suppose there is now no boy living who would do this. My boy and his brother groaned under their good resolution, I do not know how long; but the day came when they could bear it no longer, though I cannot give just the time or the terms of their backsliding. That elder brother had been hard enough on my boy before the period of this awful reform: his uprightness, his unselfishness, his truthfulness were a daily reproach to him, and it did not need this season of absolute sincerity to complete his wretchedness. Yet it was an experience which afterwards he would not willingly have missed: for once in his little confused life he had tried to practise a virtue because the opposite vice had been made to appear foolish and mischievous to him; and not from any superstitious fear or hope.

As far as I can make out, he had far more fears than hopes; and perhaps every boy has. It was in the Smith house that he began to be afraid of ghosts, though he never saw one, or anything like one. He never saw even the good genius who came down the chimney and filled the children's stockings at Christmas. He wished to see him; but he understood that St. Nicholas was a shy spirit, and was apt to pass by the stockings of boys who lay in wait for him. His mother had told him how the Peltsnickel used to come with a bundle of rods for the bad children when the Chriskingle brought the presents of the good ones, among his grandmother's Pennsylvania German kindred; and he had got them all somehow mixed up together. Then St. Nicholas, though he was so pleasant and friendly in the poem about the night before Christmas, was known to some of the neighbor boys as Santa Claus; they called it Centre Claws, and my boy imagined him with large talons radiating from the pit of his stomach. But this was all nothing to the notion of Dowd's spectacles, which his father sometimes joked him about, and which were represented by a pair of hollow, glassless iron rims which he had found in the street. They may or may not have belonged to Dowd, and Dowd may have been an Irishman in the neighborhood, or he may not; he may have died, or he may not; but there was something in the mere gruesome mention of his spectacles which related itself to all the boy had conceived of the ghostly and ghastly, and all that was alarming in the supernatural; he could never say in the least how or why. I fancy no child can ever explain just why it is affected in this way or that way by the things that are or are not in the world about it; it is not easy to do this for one's self in after-life. At any rate, it is certain that my boy dwelt most of his time amid shadows that were, perhaps, projected over his narrow outlook from some former state of being, or from the gloomy minds of long-dead ancestors. His home was cheerful and most happy, but he peopled all its nooks and corners with shapes of doom and horror. The other boys were not slow to find this out, and their invention supplied with ready suggestion of officers and prisons any little lack of misery his spectres and goblins left. He often narrowly escaped arrest, or thought so, when they built a fire in the street at night, and suddenly kicked it to pieces, and shouted, "Run, run! The constable will catch you!" Nothing but flight saved my boy, in these cases, when he was small. He grew bolder, after a while, concerning constables, but never concerning ghosts; they shivered in the autumnal evenings among the tall stalks of the corn-field that stretched, a vast wilderness, behind the house to the next street, and they walked the night everywhere.

"RUN, RUN! THE CONSTABLE WILL CATCH YOU!"

Yet nothing more tragical, that he could remember, really happened while he lived in the Smith house than something he saw one bright sunny morning, while all the boys were hanging on the fence of the next house, and watching the martins flying down to the ground from their box in the gable. The birds sent out sharp cries of terror or anger, and presently he saw a black cat crouching in the grass, with half-shut eyes and an air of dreamy indifference. The birds swept down in longer and lower loops towards the cat, drawn by some fatal charm, or by fear of the danger that threatened their colony from the mere presence of the cat; but she did not stir. Suddenly she sprang into the air, and then darted away with a martin in her mouth, while my boy's heart leaped into his own, and the other boys rushed after the cat.

As when something dreadful happens, this seemed not to have happened; but a lovely experience leaves a sense of enduring fact behind, and remains a rich possession no matter how slight and simple it was. My boy's mother has been dead almost a quarter of a century, but as one of the elder children he knew her when she was young and gay; and his last distinct association with the Smith house is of coming home with her after a visit to her mother's far up the Ohio River. In their absence the June grass, which the children's feet always kept trampled down so low, had flourished up in purple blossom, and now stood rank and tall; and the mother threw herself on her knees in it, and tossed and frolicked with her little ones like a girl. The picture remains, and the wonder of the world in which it was true once, while all the phantasmagory of spectres has long vanished away.

The boy could not recall the family's removal to the Falconer house. They were not there, and then they were there. It was a brick house, at a corner of the principal street, and in the gable there were places for mock-windows where there had never been blinds put, but where the swallows had thickly built their nests. I dare say my boy might have been willing to stone these nests, but he was not allowed, either he or his mates, who must have panted with him to improve such an opportunity of havoc. There was a real window in the gable from which he could look out of the garret; such a garret as every boy should once have the use of some time in his life. It was dim and low, though it seemed high, and the naked brown rafters were studded with wasps' nests; and the rain beat on the shingles overhead. The house had been occupied by a physician, and under the eaves the children found heaps of phials full of doctor's stuff; the garret abounded in their own family boxes and barrels, but there was always room for a swing, which the boys used in training for their circuses. Below the garret there were two unimportant stories with chambers, dining-room, parlor, and so on; then you came to the brick-paved kitchen in the basement, and a perfectly glorious cellar, with rats in it. Outside there was a large yard, with five or six huge old cherry-trees, and a garden plot, where every spring my boy tried to make a garden, with never-failing failure.

The house gave even to him a sense of space unknown before, and he could recall his mother's satisfaction in it. He has often been back there in dreams, and found it on the old scale of grandeur; but no doubt it was a very simple affair. The fortunes of a Whig editor in a place so overwhelmingly democratic as the Boy's Town were not such as could have warranted his living in a palace; and he must have been poor, as the world goes now. But the family always lived in abundance, and in their way they belonged to the employing class; that is, the father had men to work for him. On the other hand, he worked with them; and the boys, as they grew old enough, were taught to work with them, too. My boy grew old enough very young; and was put to use in the printing-office before he was ten years of age. This was not altogether because he was needed there, I dare say, but because it was part of his father's Swedenborgian philosophy that every one should fulfil a use; I do not know that when the boy wanted to go swimming, or hunting, or skating, it consoled him much to reflect that the angels in the highest heaven delighted in uses; nevertheless, it was good for him to be of use, though maybe not so much use.

If his mother did her own work, with help only now and then from a hired girl, that was the custom of the time and country; and her memory was always the more reverend to him, because whenever he looked back at her in those dim years, he saw her about some of those household offices which are so beautiful to a child. She was always the best and tenderest mother, and her love had the heavenly art of making each child feel itself the most important, while she was partial to none. In spite of her busy days she followed their father in his religion and literature, and at night, when her long toil was over, she sat with the children and listened while he read aloud. The first book my boy remembered to have heard him read was Moore's "Lalla Rookh," of which he formed but a vague notion, though while he struggled after its meaning he took all its music in, and began at once to make rhymes of his own. He had no conception of literature except the pleasure there was in making it; and he had no outlook into the world of it, which must have been pretty open to his father. The father read aloud some of Dickens's Christmas stories, then new; and the boy had a good deal of trouble with the "Haunted Man." One rarest night of all, the family sat up till two o'clock, listening to a novel that my boy long ago forgot the name of, if he ever knew its name. It was all about a will, forged or lost, and there was a great scene in court, and after that the mother declared that she could not go to bed till she heard the end. His own first reading was in history. At nine years of age he read the history of Greece, and the history of Rome, and he knew that Goldsmith wrote them. One night his father told the boys all about Don Quixote; and a little while after he gave my boy the book. He read it over and over again; but he did not suppose it was a novel. It was his elder brother who read novels, and a novel was like "Handy Andy," or "Harry Lorrequer," or the "Bride of Lammermoor." His brother had another novel which they preferred to either; it was in Harper's old "Library of Select Novels," and was called "Alamance; or, the Great and Final Experiment," and it was about the life of some sort of community in North Carolina. It bewitched them, and though my boy could not afterwards recall a single fact or figure in it, he could bring before his mind's eye every trait of its outward aspect. It was at this time that his father bought an English-Spanish grammar from a returned volunteer, who had picked it up in the city of Mexico, and gave it to the boy. He must have expected him to learn Spanish from it; but the boy did not know even the parts of speech in English. As the father had once taught English grammar in six lessons, from a broadside of his own authorship, he may have expected the principle of heredity to help the boy; and certainly he did dig the English grammar out of that blessed book, and the Spanish language with it, but after many long years, and much despair over the difference between a preposition and a substantive.

All this went along with great and continued political excitement, and with some glimpses of the social problem. It was very simple then; nobody was very rich, and nobody was in want; but somehow, as the boy grew older, he began to discover that there were differences, even in the little world about him; some were higher and some were lower. From the first he was taught by precept and example to take the side of the lower. As the children were denied oftener than they were indulged, the margin of their own abundance must have been narrower than they ever knew then; but if they had been of the most prosperous, their bent in this matter would have been the same. Once there was a church festival, or something of that sort, and there was a good deal of the provision left over, which it was decided should be given to the poor. This was very easy, but it was not so easy to find the poor whom it should be given to. At last a hard-working widow was chosen to receive it; the ladies carried it to her front door and gave it her, and she carried it to her back door and threw it into the alley. No doubt she had enough without it, but there were circumstances of indignity or patronage attending the gift which were recognized in my boy's home, and which helped afterwards to make him doubtful of all giving, except the humblest, and restive with a world in which there need be any giving at all.

III.
THE RIVER.

It seems to me that the best way to get at the heart of any boy's town is to take its different watercourses and follow them into it.

The house where my boy first lived was not far from the river, and he must have seen it often before he noticed it. But he was not aware of it till he found it under the bridge. Without the river there could not have been a bridge; the fact of the bridge may have made him look for the river; but the bridge is foremost in his mind. It is a long wooden tunnel, with two roadways, and a foot-path on either side of these; there is a toll-house at each end, and from one to the other it is about as far as from the Earth to the planet Mars. On the western shore of the river is a smaller town than the Boy's Town, and in the perspective the entrance of the bridge on that side is like a dim little doorway. The timbers are of a hugeness to strike fear into the heart of the boldest little boy; and there is something awful even about the dust in the roadways; soft and thrillingly cool to the boy's bare feet, it lies thick in a perpetual twilight, streaked at intervals by the sun that slants in at the high, narrow windows under the roof; it has a certain potent, musty smell. The bridge has three piers, and at low water hardier adventurers than he wade out to the middle pier; some heroes even fish there, standing all day on the loose rocks about the base of the pier. He shudders to see them, and aches with wonder how they will get ashore. Once he is there when a big boy wades back from the middle pier, where he has been to rob a goose's nest; he has some loose silver change in his wet hand, and my boy understands that it has come out of one of the goose eggs. This fact, which he never thought of questioning, gets mixed up in his mind with an idea of riches, of treasure-trove, in the cellar of an old house that has been torn down near the end of the bridge.

On the bridge he first saw the crazy man who belongs in every boy's town. In this one he was a hapless, harmless creature, whom the boys knew as Solomon Whistler, perhaps because his name was Whistler, perhaps because he whistled; though when my boy met him midway of the bridge, he marched swiftly and silently by, with his head high and looking neither to the right nor to the left, with an insensibility to the boy's presence that froze his blood and shrivelled him up with terror. As his fancy early became the sport of playfellows not endowed with one so vivid, he was taught to expect that Solomon Whistler would get him some day, though what he would do with him when he had got him his anguish must have been too great even to let him guess. Some of the boys said Solomon had gone crazy from fear of being drafted in the war of 1812; others that he had been crossed in love; but my boy did not quite know then what either meant. He only knew that Solomon Whistler lived at the poor-house beyond the eastern border of the town, and that he ranged between this sojourn and the illimitable wilderness north of the town on the western shore of the river. The crazy man was often in the boy's dreams, the memories of which blend so with the memories of real occurrences: he could not tell later whether he once crossed the bridge when the footway had been partly taken up, and he had to walk on the girders, or whether he only dreamed of that awful passage. It was quite fearful enough to cross when the footway was all down, and he could see the blue gleam of the river far underneath through the cracks between the boards. It made his brain reel; and he felt that he took his life in his hand whenever he entered the bridge, even when he had grown old enough to be making an excursion with some of his playmates to the farm of an uncle of theirs who lived two miles up the river. The farmer gave them all the watermelons they wanted to eat, and on the way home, when they lay resting under the sycamores on the river-bank, Solomon Whistler passed by in the middle of the road, silent, swift, straight onward. I do not know why the sight of this afflicted soul did not slay my boy on the spot, he was so afraid of him; but the crazy man never really hurt any one, though the boys followed and mocked him as soon as he got by.

The boys knew little or nothing of the river south of the bridge, and frequented mainly that mile-long stretch of it between the bridge and the dam, beyond which there was practically nothing for many years; afterwards they came to know that this strange region was inhabited. Just above the bridge the Hydraulic emptied into the river with a heart-shaking plunge over an immense mill-wheel; and there was a cluster of mills at this point, which were useful in accumulating the waters into fishing-holes before they rushed through the gates upon the wheel. The boys used to play inside the big mill-wheel before the water was let into the Hydraulic, and my boy caught his first fish in the pool below the wheel. The mills had some secondary use in making flour and the like, but this could not concern a small boy. They were as simply a part of his natural circumstance as the large cottonwood-tree which hung over the river from a point near by, and which seemed to have always an oriole singing in it. All along there the banks were rather steep, and to him they looked very high. The blue clay that formed them was full of springs, which the boys dammed up in little ponds and let loose in glassy falls upon their flutter-mills. As with everything that boys do, these mills were mostly failures; the pins which supported the wheels were always giving way; and though there were instances of boys who started their wheels at recess and found them still fluttering away at noon when they came out of school, none ever carried his enterprise so far as to spin the cotton blowing from the balls of the cottonwood-tree by the shore, as they all meant to do. They met such disappointments with dauntless cheerfulness, and lightly turned from some bursting bubble to some other where the glory of the universe was still mirrored. The river shore was strewn not only with waste cotton, but with drift which the water had made porous, and which they called smoke-wood. They made cigars for their own use out of it, and it seemed to them that it might be generally introduced as a cheap and simple substitute for tobacco; but they never got any of it into the market, not even the market of that world where the currency was pins.

The river had its own climate, and this climate was of course much such a climate as the boys, for whom nature intended the river, would have chosen. I do not believe it was ever winter there, though it was sometimes late autumn, so that the boys could have some use for the caves they dug at the top of the bank, with a hole coming through the turf, to let out the smoke of the fires they built inside. They had the joy of choking and blackening over these flues, and they intended to live on corn and potatoes borrowed from the household stores of the boy whose house was nearest. They never got so far as to parch the corn or to bake the potatoes in their caves, but there was the fire, and the draft was magnificent. The light of the red flames painted the little, happy, foolish faces, so long since wrinkled and grizzled with age, or mouldered away to dust, as the boys huddled before them under the bank, and fed them with the drift, or stood patient of the heat and cold in the afternoon light of some vast Saturday waning to nightfall.

The river-climate, with these autumnal intervals, was made up of a quick, eventful springtime, followed by the calm of a cloudless summer that seemed never to end. But the spring, short as it was, had its great attractions, and chief of these was the freshet which it brought to the river. They would hear somehow that the river was rising, and then the boys, who had never connected its rise with the rains they must have been having, would all go down to its banks and watch the swelling waters. These would be yellow and thick, and the boiling current would have smooth, oily eddies, where pieces of drift would whirl round and round, and then escape and slip down the stream. There were saw-logs and whole trees with their branching tops, lengths of fence and hen-coops and pig-pens; once there was a stable; and if the flood continued, there began to come swollen bodies of horses and cattle. This must have meant serious loss to the people living on the river-bottoms above, but the boys counted it all gain. They cheered the objects as they floated by, and they were breathless with the excitement of seeing the men who caught fence-rails and cord-wood, and even saw-logs, with iron prongs at the points of long poles, as they stood on some jutting point of shore and stretched far out over the flood. The boys exulted in the turbid spread of the stream, which filled its low western banks and stole over their tops, and washed into all the hollow places along its shores, and shone among the trunks of the sycamores on Delorac's Island, which was almost of the geographical importance of The Island in Old River. When the water began to go down their hearts sank with it; and they gave up the hope of seeing the bridge carried away. Once the river rose to within a few feet of it, so that if the right piece of drift had been there to do its duty, the bridge might have been torn from its piers and swept down the raging tide into those unknown gulfs to the southward. Many a time they went to bed full of hope that it would at least happen in the night, and woke to learn with shame and grief in the morning that the bridge was still there, and the river was falling. It was a little comfort to know that some of the big boys had almost seen it go, watching as far into the night as nine o'clock with the men who sat up near the bridge till daylight: men of leisure and public spirit, but not perhaps the leading citizens.

There must have been a tedious time between the going down of the flood and the first days when the water was warm enough for swimming; but it left no trace. The boys are standing on the shore while the freshet rushes by, and then they are in the water, splashing, diving, ducking; it is like that; so that I do not know just how to get in that period of fishing which must always have come between. There were not many fish in that part of the Miami; my boy's experience was full of the ignominy of catching shiners and suckers, or, at the best, mudcats, as they called the yellow catfish; but there were boys, of those who cursed and swore, who caught sunfish, as they called the bream; and there were men who were reputed to catch at will, as it were, silvercats and river-bass. They fished with minnows, which they kept in battered tin buckets that they did not allow you even to touch, or hardly to look at; my boy scarcely breathed in their presence; when one of them got up to cast his line in a new place, the boys all ran, and then came slowly back. These men often carried a flask of liquid that had the property, when taken inwardly, of keeping the damp out. The boys respected them for their ability to drink whiskey, and thought it a fit and honorable thing that they should now and then fall into the river over the brinks where they had set their poles.

But they disappear like persons in a dream, and their fishing-time vanishes with them, and the swimming-time is in full possession of the river, and of all the other waters of the Boy's Town. The river, the Canal Basin, the Hydraulic and its Reservoirs, seemed all full of boys at the same moment; but perhaps it was not the same, for my boy was always in each place, and so he must have been there at different times. Each place had its delights and advantages, but the swimming-holes in the river were the greatest favorites. He could not remember when he began to go into them, though it certainly was before he could swim. There was a time when he was afraid of getting in over his head; but he did not know just when he learned to swim, any more than he knew when he learned to read; he could not swim, and then he could swim; he could not read, and then he could read; but I dare say the reading came somewhat before the swimming. Yet the swimming must have come very early, and certainly it was kept up with continual practice; he swam quite as much as he read; perhaps more. The boys had deep swimming-holes and shallow ones; and over the deep ones there was always a spring-board, from which they threw somersaults, or dived straight down into the depths, where there were warm and cold currents mysteriously interwoven. They believed that these deep holes were infested by water-snakes, though they never saw any, and they expected to be bitten by snapping-turtles, though this never happened. Fiery dragons could not have kept them out; gallynippers, whatever they were, certainly did not; they were believed to abound at the bottom of the deep holes; but the boys never stayed long in the deep holes, and they preferred the shallow places, where the river broke into a long ripple (they called it riffle) on its gravelly bed, and where they could at once soak and bask in the musical rush of the sunlit waters. I have heard people in New England blame all the Western rivers for being yellow and turbid; but I know that after the spring floods, when the Miami had settled down to its summer business with the boys, it was as clear and as blue as if it were spilled out of the summer sky. The boys liked the riffle because they could stay in so long there, and there were little landlocked pools and shallows, where the water was even warmer, and they could stay in longer. At most places under the banks there was clay of different colors, which they used for war-paint in their Indian fights; and after they had their Indian fights they could rush screaming and clattering into the riffle. When the stream had washed them clean down to their red sunburn or their leathern tan, they could paint up again and have more Indian fights.

I do not know why my boy's associations with Delorac's Island were especially wild in their character, for nothing more like outlawry than the game of mumble-the-peg ever occurred there. Perhaps it was because the boys had to get to it by water that it seemed beyond the bounds of civilization. They might have reached it by the bridge, but the temper of the boys on the western shore was uncertain; they would have had to run the gauntlet of their river-guard on the way up to it; and they might have been friendly or they might not; it would have depended a good deal on the size and number of the interlopers. Besides, it was more glorious to wade across to the island from their side of the river. They undressed and gathered their clothes up into a bundle, which they put on their heads and held there with one hand, while they used the other for swimming, when they came to a place beyond their depth. Then they dressed again, and stretched themselves under the cottonwood-trees and sycamores, and played games and told stories, and longed for a gun to kill the blackbirds which nested in the high tops, and at nightfall made such a clamor in getting to roost that it almost deafened you.

My boy never distinctly knew what formed that island, but as there was a mill there, it must have been made by the mill-race leaving and rejoining the river. It was enough for him to know that the island was there, and that a parrot—a screaming, whistling, and laughing parrot, which was a Pretty Poll, and always Wanted a Cracker—dwelt in a pretty cottage, almost hidden in trees, just below the end of the island. This parrot had the old Creole gentleman living with it who owned the island, and whom it had brought from New Orleans. The boys met him now and then as he walked abroad, with a stick, and his large stomach bowed in front of him. For no reason under the sun they were afraid of him; perhaps they thought he resented their parleys with the parrot. But he and the parrot existed solely to amuse and to frighten them; and on their own side of the river, just opposite the island, there were established some small industries for their entertainment and advantage, on a branch of the Hydraulic. I do not know just what it was they did with a mustard-mill that was there, but the turning-shop supplied them with a deep bed of elastic shavings just under the bank, which they turned somersaults into, when they were not turning them into the river.

I wonder what sign the boys who read this have for challenging or inviting one another to go in swimming. The boys in the Boy's Town used to make the motion of swimming with both arms; or they held up the forefinger and middle-finger in the form of a swallow-tail; they did this when it was necessary to be secret about it, as in school, and when they did not want the whole crowd of boys to come along; and often when they just pretended they did not want some one to know. They really had to be secret at times, for some of the boys were not allowed to go in at all; others were forbidden to go in more than once or twice a day; and as they all *had* to go in at least three or four times a day, some sort of sign had to be used that was understood among themselves alone. Since this is a true history, I had better own that they nearly all, at one time or other, must have told lies about it, either before or after the fact, some habitually, some only in great extremity. Here and there a boy, like my boy's elder brother, would not tell lies at all, even about going in swimming; but by far the greater number bowed to their hard fate, and told them. They promised that they would not go in, and then they said that they had not been in; but Sin, for which they had made this sacrifice, was apt to betray them. Either they got their shirts on wrong side out in dressing, or else, while they were in, some enemy came upon them and tied their shirts. There are few cruelties which public opinion in the boys' world condemns, but I am glad to remember, to their honor, that there were not many in that Boy's Town who would tie shirts; and I fervently hope that there is no boy now living who would do it. As the crime is probably extinct, I will say that in those wicked days, if you were such a miscreant, and there was some boy you hated, you stole up and tied the hardest kind of a knot in one arm or both arms of his shirt. Then, if the Evil One put it into your heart, you soaked the knot in water, and pounded it with a stone.

I am glad to know that in the days when he was thoughtless and senseless enough, my boy never was guilty of any degree of this meanness. It was his brother, I suppose, who taught him to abhor it; and perhaps it was his own suffering from it in part; for he, too, sometimes shed bitter tears over such a knot, as I have seen hapless little wretches do, tearing at it with their nails and gnawing at it with their teeth, knowing that the time was passing when they could hope to hide the fact that they had been in swimming, and foreseeing no remedy but to cut off the sleeve above the knot, or else put on their clothes without the shirt, and trust to untying the knot when it got dry.

There must have been a lurking anxiety in all the boys' hearts when they went in without leave, or, as my boy was apt to do, when explicitly forbidden. He was not apt at lying, I dare say, and so he took the course of open disobedience. He could not see the danger that filled the home hearts with fear for him, and he must have often broken the law and been forgiven, before Justice one day appeared for him on the river-bank and called him away from his stolen joys. It was an awful moment, and it covered him with shame before his mates, who heartlessly rejoiced, as children do, in the doom which they are escaping. That sin, at least, he fully expiated; and I will whisper to the Young People here at the end of the chapter, that somehow, soon or late, our sins do overtake us, and insist upon being paid for. That is not the best reason for not sinning, but it is well to know it, and to believe it in our acts as well as our thoughts. You will find people to tell you that things only happen so and so. It may be; only, I know that no good thing ever happened to happen to me when I had done wrong.

IV.
THE CANAL AND ITS BASIN.

The canal came from Lake Erie, two hundred miles to the northward, and joined the Ohio River twenty miles south of the Boy's Town. For a time my boy's father was collector of tolls on it, but even when he was old enough to understand that his father held this State office (the canal belonged to the State) because he had been such a good Whig, and published the Whig newspaper, he could not grasp the notion of the distance which the canal-boats came out of and went into. He saw them come and he saw them go; he did not ask whence or whither; his wonder, if he had any about them, did not go beyond the second lock. It was hard enough to get it to the head of the Basin, which left the canal half a mile or so to the eastward, and stretched down into the town, a sheet of smooth water, fifteen or twenty feet deep, and a hundred wide; his sense ached with, the effort of conceiving of the other side of it. The Basin was bordered on either side near the end by pork-houses, where the pork was cut up and packed, and then lay in long rows of barrels on the banks, with other long rows of salt-barrels, and yet other long rows of whiskey-barrels; cooper-shops, where the barrels were made, alternated with the pork-houses. The boats brought the salt and carried away the pork and whiskey; but the boy's practical knowledge of them was that they lay there for the boys to dive off of when they went in swimming, and to fish under. The water made a soft tuck-tucking at the sterns of the boat, and you could catch sunfish, if you were the right kind of a boy, or the wrong kind; the luck seemed to go a good deal with boys who were not good for much else. Some of the boats were open their whole length, with a little cabin at the stern, and these pretended to be for carrying wood and stone, but really again were for the use of the boys after a hard rain, when they held a good deal of water, and you could pole yourself up and down on the loose planks in them. The boys formed the notion at times that some of these boats were abandoned by their owners, and they were apt to be surprised by their sudden return. A feeling of transgression was mixed up with the joys of this kind of navigation; perhaps some of the boys were forbidden it. No limit was placed on their swimming in the Basin, except that of the law which prohibited it in the daytime, as the Basin was quite in the heart of the town. In the warm summer nights of that southerly latitude, the water swarmed with laughing, shouting, screaming boys, who plunged from the banks and rioted in the delicious water, diving and ducking, flying and following, safe in the art of swimming which all of them knew. They turned somersaults from the decks of the canal-boats; some of the boys could turn double somersaults, and one boy got so far as to turn a somersault and a half; it was long before the time of electric lighting, but when he struck the water there came a flash that seemed to illumine the universe.

I am afraid that the Young People will think I am telling them too much about swimming. But in the Boy's Town the boys really led a kind of amphibious life, and as long as the long summer lasted they were almost as much in the water as on the land. The Basin, however, unlike the river, had a winter as well as a summer climate, and one of the very first things that my boy could remember was being on the ice there, when a young man caught him up into his arms, and skated off with him almost as far away as the canal. He remembered the fearful joy of the adventure, and the pride, too; for he had somehow the notion that this young fellow was handsome and fine, and did him an honor by his notice—so soon does some dim notion of worldly splendor turn us into snobs! The next thing was his own attempt at skating, when he was set down from the bank by his brother, full of a vainglorious confidence in his powers, and appeared instantly to strike on the top of his head. Afterwards he learned to skate, but he did not know when, any more than he knew just the moment of learning to read or to swim. He became passionately fond of skating, and kept at it all day long when there was ice for it, which was not often in those soft winters. They made a very little ice go a long way in the Boy's Town; and began to use it for skating as soon as there was a glazing of it on the Basin. None of them ever got drowned there; though a boy would often start from one bank and go flying to the other, trusting his speed to save him, while the thin sheet sank and swayed, but never actually broke under him. Usually the ice was not thick enough to have a fire built on it; and it must have been on ice which was just strong enough to bear that my boy skated all one bitter afternoon at Old River, without a fire to warm by. At first his feet were very cold, and then they gradually felt less cold, and at last he did not feel them at all. He thought this very nice, and he told one of the big boys. "Why, your feet are frozen!" said the big boy, and he dragged off my boy's skates, and the little one ran all the long mile home, crazed with terror, and not knowing what moment his feet might drop off there in the road. His mother plunged them in a bowl of ice-cold water, and then rubbed them with flannel, and so thawed them out; but that could not save him from the pain of their coming to: it was intense, and there must have been a time afterwards when he did not use his feet.

His skates themselves were of a sort that I am afraid boys would smile at nowadays. When you went to get a pair of skates forty or fifty years ago, you did not make your choice between a Barney & Berry and an Acme, which fastened on with the turn of a screw or the twist of a clamp. You found an assortment of big and little sizes of solid wood bodies with guttered blades turning up in front with a sharp point, or perhaps curling over above the toe. In this case they sometimes ended in an acorn; if this acorn was of brass, it transfigured the boy who wore that skate; he might have been otherwise all rags and patches, but the brass acorn made him splendid from head to foot. When you had bought your skates, you took them to a carpenter, and stood awe-strickenly about while he pierced the wood with strap-holes; or else you managed to bore them through with a hot iron yourself. Then you took them to a saddler, and got him to make straps for them; that is, if you were rich, and your father let you have a quarter to pay for the job. If not, you put strings through, and tied your skates on. They were always coming off, or getting crosswise of your foot, or feeble-mindedly slumping down on one side of the wood; but it did not matter, if you had a fire on the ice, fed with old barrels and boards and cooper's shavings, and could sit round it with your skates on, and talk and tell stories, between your flights and races afar; and come whizzing back to it from the frozen distance, and glide, with one foot lifted, almost among the embers.

Beyond the pork-houses, and up farther towards the canal, there were some houses under the Basin banks. They were good places for the fever-and-ague which people had in those days without knowing it was malaria, or suffering it to interfere much with the pleasure and business of life; but they seemed to my boy bowers of delight, especially one where there was a bear, chained to a weeping-willow, and another where there was a fishpond with gold-fish in it. He expected this bear to get loose and eat him, but that could not spoil his pleasure in seeing the bear stand on his hind-legs and open his red mouth, as I have seen bears do when you wound them up by a keyhole in the side. In fact, a toy bear is very much like a real bear, and safer to have round. The boys were always wanting to go and look at this bear, but he was not so exciting as the daily arrival of the Dayton packet. To my boy's young vision this craft was of such incomparable lightness and grace as no yacht of Mr. Burgess's could rival. When she came in of a summer evening her deck was thronged with people, and the captain stood with his right foot on the spring-catch that held the tow-rope. The water curled away on either side of her sharp prow, that cut its way onward at the full rate of five miles an hour, and the team came swinging down the tow-path at a gallant trot, the driver sitting the hindmost horse of three, and cracking his long-lashed whip with loud explosions, as he whirled its snaky spirals in the air. All the boys in town were there, meekly proud to be ordered out of his way, to break and fly before his volleyed oaths and far before his horses' feet; and suddenly the captain pressed his foot on the spring and released the tow-rope. The driver kept on to the stable with unslackened speed, and the line followed him, swishing and skating over the water, while the steersman put his helm hard aport, and the packet rounded to, and swam softly and slowly up to her moorings. No steamer arrives from Europe now with such thrilling majesty.

The canal-boatmen were all an heroic race, and the boys humbly hoped that some day, if they proved worthy, they might grow up to be drivers; not indeed packet-drivers; they were not so conceited as that; but freight-boat drivers, of two horses, perhaps, but gladly of one. High or low, the drivers had a great deal of leisure, which commended their calling to the boyish fancy; and my boy saw them, with a longing to speak to them, even to approach them, never satisfied, while they amused the long summer afternoon in the shade of the tavern by a game of skill peculiar to them. They put a tack into a whiplash, and then, whirling it round and round, drove it to the head in a target marked out on the weather-boarding. Some of them had a perfect aim; and in fact it was a very pretty feat, and well worth seeing.

Another feat, which the pioneers of the region had probably learned from the Indians, was throwing the axe. The thrower caught the axe by the end of the helve, and with a dextrous twirl sent it flying through the air, and struck its edge into whatever object he aimed at—usually a tree. Two of the Basin loafers were brothers, and they were always quarrelling and often fighting. One was of the unhappy fraternity of town-drunkards, and somehow the boys thought him a finer fellow than the other, whom somehow they considered "mean," and they were always of his side in their controversies. One afternoon these brothers quarrelled a long time, and then the sober brother retired to the doorway of a pork-house, where he stood, probably brooding upon his injuries, when the drunkard, who had remained near the tavern, suddenly caught up an axe and flung it; the boys saw it sail across the corner of the Basin, and strike in the door just above his brother's head. This one did not lose an instant; while the axe still quivered in the wood, he hurled himself upon the drunkard, and did that justice on him which he would not ask from the law, perhaps because it was a family affair; perhaps because those wretched men were no more under the law than the boys were.

I do not mean that there was no law for the boys, for it was manifest to their terror in two officers whom they knew as constables, and who may have reigned one after another, or together, with full power of life and death over them, as they felt; but who in a community mainly so peaceful acted upon Dogberry's advice, and made and meddled with rogues as little as they could. From time to time it was known among the boys that you would be taken up if you went in swimming inside of the corporation line, and for a while they would be careful to keep beyond it; but this could not last; they were soon back in the old places, and I suppose no arrests were ever really made. They did, indeed, hear once that Old Griffin, as they called him, caught a certain boy in the river before dark, and carried him up through the town to his own home naked. Of course no such thing ever happened; but the boys believed it, and it froze my boy's soul with fear; all the more because this constable was a cabinet-maker and made coffins; from his father's printing-office the boy could hear the long slide of his plane over the wood, and he could smell the varnish on the boards.

I dare say Old Griffin was a kindly man enough, and not very old; and I suppose that the other constable, as known to his family and friends, was not at all the gloomy headsman he appeared to the boys. When he became constable (they had not the least notion how a man became constable) they heard that his rule was to be marked by unwonted severity against the crime of going in swimming inside the corporation line, and so they kept strictly to the letter of the law. But one day some of them found themselves in the water beyond the First Lock, when the constable appeared on the towpath, suddenly, as if he and his horse had come up out of the ground. He told them that he had got them now, and he ordered them to come along with him; he remained there amusing himself with their tears, their prayers, and then vanished again. Heaven knows how they lived through it; but they must have got safely home in the usual way, and life must have gone on as before. No doubt the man did not realize the torture he put them to; but it was a cruel thing; and I never have any patience with people who exaggerate a child's offence to it, and make it feel itself a wicked criminal for some little act of scarcely any consequence. If we elders stand here in the place of the Heavenly Father towards those younger children of His, He will not hold us guiltless when we obscure for them the important difference between a great and a small misdeed, or wring their souls, fear-clouded as they always are, with a sense of perdition for no real sin.

THE SIX-MILE LEVEL.

"HE TOLD THEM THAT HE HAD GOT THEM NOW."

V.

THE HYDRAULIC AND ITS RESERVOIRS.—OLD RIVER.

There were two branches of the Hydraulic: one followed the course of the Miami, from some unknown point to the northward, on the level of its high bank, and joined the other where it emptied into the river just above the bridge. This last came down what had been a street, and it must have been very pretty to have these two swift streams of clear water rushing through the little town, under the culverts, and between the stone walls of its banks. But what a boy mainly cares for in a thing is *use*, and the boys tried to make some use of the Hydraulic, since it was there to find what they could do with it. Of course they were aware of the mills dotted along its course, and they knew that it ran them; but I do not believe any of them thought that it was built merely to run flour-mills and saw-mills and cotton-mills. They did what they could to find out its real use, but they could make very little of it. The current was so rapid that it would not freeze in winter, and in summer they could not go in swimming in it by day, because it was so public, and at night the Basin had more attractions. There was danger of cutting your feet on the broken glass and crockery which people threw into the Hydraulic, and though the edges of the culverts were good for jumping off of, the boys did not find them of much practical value. Sometimes you could catch sunfish in the Hydraulic, but it was generally too swift, and the only thing you could depend upon was catching crawfish. These abounded so that if you dropped a string with a bit of meat on it into the water anywhere, you could pull it up again with two or three crawfish hanging to it. The boys could not begin to use them all for bait, which was the only use their Creator seemed to have designed them for; but they had vaguely understood that people somewhere ate them, or something like them, though they had never known even the name of lobsters; and they always intended to get their mothers to have them cooked for them. None of them ever did.

They could sometimes, under high favor of fortune, push a dog into the Hydraulic, or get him to jump in after a stick; and then have the excitement of following him from one culvert to another, till he found a foothold and scrambled out. Once my boy saw a chicken cock sailing serenely down the currant; he was told that he had been given brandy, and that brandy would enable a chicken to swim; but probably this was not true. Another time, a tremendous time, a boy was standing at the brink of a culvert, when one of his mates dared another to push him in. In those days the boys attached peculiar ideas of dishonor to taking a dare. They said, and in some sort they believed, that a boy who would take a dare would steal sheep. I do not now see why this should follow. In this case, the high spirit who was challenged felt nothing base in running up behind his unsuspecting friend and popping him into the water, and I have no doubt the victim considered the affair in the right light when he found that it was a dare. He drifted under the culvert, and when he came out he swiftly scaled the wall below, and took after the boy who had pushed him in; of course this one had the start. No great harm was done; everybody could swim, and a boy's summer costume in that hot climate was made up of a shirt and trousers and a straw hat; no boy who had any regard for his social standing wore shoes or stockings, and as they were all pretty proud, they all went barefoot from April till October.

The custom of going barefoot must have come from the South, where it used to be so common, and also from the primitive pioneer times which were so near my boy's time, fifty years ago. The South characterized the thinking and feeling of the Boy's Town, far more than the North. Most of the people were of Southern extraction, from Kentucky or Virginia, when they were not from Pennsylvania or New Jersey. There might have been other New England families, but the boys only knew of one—that of the blacksmith whose shop they liked to haunt. His children were heard to dispute about an animal they had seen, and one of them said, "Tell ye 'twa'n't a squeerrel; 'twas a maouse;" and the boys had that for a by-word. They despised Yankees as a mean-spirited race, who were stingy and would cheat; and would not hit you if you told them they lied. A person must always hit a person who told him he lied; but even if you called a Yankee a *fighting* liar (the worst form of this insult), he would not hit you, but just call you a liar back. My boy long accepted these ideas of New England as truly representative of the sectional character. Perhaps they were as fair as some ideas of the West which he afterwards found entertained in New England; but they were false and stupid all the same.

If the boys could do little with the Hydraulic, they were at no loss in regard to the Reservoirs, into which its feeding waters were gathered and held in reserve, I suppose, against a time of drought. There was the Little Reservoir first, and then a mile beyond it the Big Reservoir, and there was nearly always a large flat boat on each which was used for repairing the banks, but which the boys employed as a pleasure-barge. It seemed in some natural way to belong to them, and yet they had a feeling of something clandestine in pushing out on the Reservoir in it. Once they filled its broad, shallow hold with straw from a neighboring oatfield, and spent a long golden afternoon in simply lying under the hot September sun, in the middle of the Reservoir, and telling stories. My boy then learned, for the first time, that there was such a book as the "Arabian Nights;" one of the other boys told stories out of it, and he inferred that the sole copy in existence belonged to this boy. He knew that they all had school-books alike, but it did not occur to him that a book which was not a Reader or a Speller was ever duplicated. They did nothing with their boat except loll in it and tell stories, and as there was no current in the Reservoir, they must have remained pretty much in the same place; but they had a sense of the wildest adventure, which mounted to frenzy, when some men rose out of the earth on the shore, and shouted at them, "Hello, there! What are you doing with that boat?" They must have had an oar; at any rate, they got to the opposite bank, and, springing to land, fled somewhere into the vaguest past.

The boys went in swimming in the Little Reservoir when they were not in the River or the Basin; and they fished in the Big Reservoir, where the sunfish bit eagerly. There were large trees standing in the hollow which became the bed of the Reservoir, and these died when the water was let in around them, and gave the stretch of quiet waters a strange, weird look; about their bases was the best kind of place for sunfish, and even for bass. Of course the boys never caught any bass; that honor was reserved for men of the kind I have mentioned. It was several years before the catfish got in, and then they were mud-cats; but the boys had great luck with sunfish there and in the pools about the flood-gates, where there was always some leakage, and where my boy once caught a whole string of live fish which had got away from some other boy, perhaps weeks before; they were all swimming about, in a lively way, and the largest hungrily took his bait. The great pleasure of fishing in these pools was that the waters were so clear you could see the fat, gleaming fellows at the bottom, nosing round your hook, and going off and coming back several times before they made up their minds to bite. It seems now impossible that my boy could ever have taken pleasure in the capture of these poor creatures. I know that there are grown people, and very good, kind men, too, who defend and celebrate the sport, and value themselves on their skill in it; but I think it tolerable only in boys, who are cruel because they are thoughtless. It is not probable that any lower organism

"In corporal sufferance feels a pang as great
As when a giant dies,"

but still, I believe that even a fish knows a dumb agony from the barbs of the hook which would take somewhat from the captor's joy if he could but realize it.

"THAT HONOR WAS RESERVED FOR MEN OF THE KIND I HAVE MENTIONED."

There was, of course, a time when the Hydraulic and the Reservoirs were not where they afterwards appeared always to have been. My boy could dimly recall the day when the water was first let into the Hydraulic, and the little fellows ran along its sides to keep abreast of the current, as they easily could; and he could see more vividly the tumult which a break in the embankment of the Little Reservoir caused. The whole town rushed to the spot, or at least all the boys in it did, and a great force of men besides, with shovels and wheelbarrows, and bundles of brush and straw, and heavy logs, and heaped them into the crevasse, and piled earth on them. The men threw off their coats and all joined in the work; a great local politician led off in his shirt-sleeves; and it was as if my boy should now see the Emperor of Germany in his shirt-sleeves pushing a wheelbarrow, so high above all other men had that exalted Whig always been to him. But the Hydraulic, I believe, was a town work, and everybody felt himself an owner in it, and hoped to share in the prosperity which it should bring to all. It made the people so far one family, as every public work which they own in common always does; it made them brothers and equals, as private property never does.

Of course the boys rose to no such conception of the fact before their eyes. I suspect that in their secret hearts they would have been glad to have seen that whole embankment washed away, for the excitement's sake, and for the hope of catching the fish that would be left flopping at the bottom of the Reservoir when the waters were drained out, I think that these waters were brought somehow from Old River, but I am not sure how. Old River was very far away, and my boy was never there much, and knew little of the weird region it bounded. Once he went in swimming in it, but the still, clear waters were strangely cold, and not like those of the friendly Miami. Once, also, when the boys had gone into the vast woods of that measureless continent which they called the Island, for pawpaws or for hickory-nuts, or maybe buckeyes, they got lost; and while they ran about in terror, they heard the distant lowing and bellowing of cattle. They knew somehow, as boys know everything, that the leader of the herd, which ranged those woods in a half-savage freedom, was a vicious bull, and as the lowing and bellowing sounded nearer, they huddled together in the wildest dismay. Some were for running, some for getting over a fence near by; but they could not tell which side of the fence the herd was on. In the primitive piety of childhood my boy suggested prayer as something that had served people in extremity, and he believed that it was the only hope left. Another boy laughed, and began to climb a tree; the rest, who had received my boy's suggestion favorably, instantly followed his example; in fact, he climbed a tree himself. The herd came slowly up, and when they reached the boys' refuge they behaved with all the fury that could have been expected—they trampled and tossed the bags that held the pawpaws or buckeyes or hickory-nuts; they gored the trees where the boys hung trembling; they pawed and tossed the soft earth below; and then they must have gone away, and given them up as hopeless. My boy never had the least notion how he got home; and I dare say he was very young when he began these excursions to the woods.

In some places Old River was a stagnant pool, covered with thick green scum, and filled with frogs. The son of one of the tavern-keepers was skilled in catching them, and I fancy supplied them to his father's table; the important fact was his taking them, which he did by baiting a cluster of three hooks with red flannel, and dropping them at the end of a fish-line before a frog. The fated croaker plunged at the brilliant bait, and was caught in the breast; even as a small boy, my boy thought it a cruel sight. The boys pretended that the old frogs said, whenever this frog-catching boy came in sight, "Here comes Hawkins!—here comes Hawkins! Look out!—look out!" and a row of boys, perched on a log in the water, would sound this warning in mockery of the frogs or their foe, and plump one after another in the depths, as frogs follow their leader in swift succession. They had nothing against Hawkins. They all liked him, for he was a droll, good-natured fellow, always up to some pleasantry. One day he laughed out in school. "Was that you laughed, Henry?" asked the teacher, with unerring suspicion. "I was only smiling, Mr. Slack." "The next time, see that you don't smile so loud," said Mr. Slack, and forgave him, as any one who saw his honest face must have wished to do. They called him Old Hawkins, for fondness; and while my boy shuddered at him for his way of catching frogs, he was in love with him for his laughing eyes and the kindly ways he had, especially with the little boys.

VI.
SCHOOLS AND TEACHERS.
My boy had not a great deal to do with schools after his docile childhood. When he began to run wild with the other boys he preferred their savage freedom; and he got out of going to school by most of the devices they used. He had never quite the hardihood to play truant, but he was subject to sudden attacks of sickness, which came on about school-time and went off towards the middle of the forenoon or afternoon in a very strange manner. I suppose that such complaints are unknown at the present time, but the Young People's fathers can tell them how much suffering they used to cause among boys. At the age when my boy was beginning to outgrow them he was taken into his father's printing-office, and he completed his recovery and his education there. But all through the years when he lived in the Boy's Town he had intervals of schooling, which broke in upon the swimming and the skating, of course, but were not altogether unpleasant or unprofitable.

They began, as they are apt to do, with lessons in a private house, where a lady taught several other children, and where he possibly learned to read; though he could only remember being set on a platform in punishment for some forgotten offence. After that he went to school in the basement of a church, where a number of boys and girls were taught by a master who knew how to endear study at least to my boy. There was a garden outside of the schoolroom; hollyhocks grew in it, and the boys gathered the little cheeses, as they called the seed-buttons which form when the flowers drop off, and ate them, because boys will eat anything, and not because they liked them. With the fact of this garden is mixed a sense of drowsy heat and summer light, and that is all, except the blackboard at the end of the room and a big girl doing sums at it; and the wonder why the teacher smiled when he read in one of the girls' compositions a phrase about forging puddings and pies; my boy did not know what forging meant, so he must have been very young. But he had a zeal for learning, and somehow he took a prize in geography—a science in which he was never afterwards remarkable. The prize was a little history of Lexington, Mass., which the teacher gave him, perhaps because Lexington may have been his native town; but the history must have been very dryly told, for not a fact of it remained in the boy's mind. He was vaguely disappointed in the book, but he valued it for the teacher's sake whom he was secretly very fond of, and who had no doubt won the child's heart by some flattering notice. He thought it a great happiness to follow him, when the teacher gave up this school, and took charge of one of the public schools; but it was not the same there; the teacher could not distinguish him in that multitude of boys and girls. He did himself a little honor in spelling, but he won no praise, and he disgraced himself then as always in arithmetic. He sank into the common herd of mediocrities; and then, when his family went to live in another part of the town, he began to go to another school. He had felt that the teacher belonged to him, and it must have been a pang to find him so estranged. But he was a kind man, and long afterwards he had a friendly smile and word for the boy when they met; and then all at once he ceased to be, as men and things do in a boy's world.

The other school was another private school; and it was doubtless a school of high grade in some things, for it was called the Academy. But there was provision for the youngest beginners in a lower room, and for a while my boy went there. Before school opened in the afternoon, the children tried to roast apples on the stove, but there never was time, and they had to eat them half raw. In the singing-class there was a boy who wore his hair so enviably long that he could toss it on his neck as he wheeled in the march of the class round the room; his father kept a store and he brought candy to school. They sang "Scotland's burning! Pour on water" and "Home, home! Dearest and happiest home!" No doubt they did other things, but none of them remained in my boy's mind; and when he was promoted to the upper room very little more was added. He studied Philosophy, as it was called, and he learned, as much from the picture as the text, that you could not make a boat go by filling her sail from bellows on board; he did not see why. But he was chiefly concerned with his fears about the Chemical Room, where I suppose some chemical apparatus must have been kept, but where the big boys were taken to be whipped. It was a place of dreadful execution to him, and when he was once sent to the Chemical Boom, and shut up there, because he was crying, and because, as he explained, he could not stop crying without a handkerchief, and he had none with him, he never expected to come out alive.

In fact, as I have said, he dwelt in a world of terrors; and I doubt if some of the big boys who were taken there to be whipped underwent so much as he in being merely taken to the place where they had been whipped. At the same time, while he cowered along in the shadow of unreal dangers, he had a boy's boldness with most of the real ones, and he knew how to resent an indignity even at the hands of the teacher who could send him to the Chemical Room at pleasure. He knew what belonged to him as a small boy of honor, and one thing was, not to be tamely put back from a higher to a lower place in his studies. I dare say that boys do not mind this now; they must have grown ever so much wiser since my boy went to school; but in his time, when you were put back, say from the Third Reader to the Second Reader, you took your books and left school. That was what the other boys expected of you, and it was the only thing for you to do if you had the least self-respect, for you were put back to the Second Reader after having failed to read the Third, and it was a public shame which nothing but leaving that school could wipe out.

The other boys would have a right to mock you if you did not do it; and as soon as the class was dismissed you went to your desk as haughtily as you could, and began putting your books and your slate and your inkstand together, with defiant glances at the teacher; and then when twelve o'clock came, or four o'clock, and the school was let out, you tucked the bundle under your arm and marched out of the room, with as much majesty as could be made to comport with a chip hat and bare feet; and as you passed the teacher you gave a twist of the head that was meant to carry dismay to the heart of your enemy. I note all these particulars carefully, so as to show the boys of the present day what fools the boys of the past were; though I think they will hardly believe it. My boy was once that kind of fool; but not twice. He left school with all his things at twelve o'clock, and he returned with them at one; for his father and mother did not agree with him about the teacher's behavior in putting him back. No boy's father and mother agreed with him on this point; every boy returned in just the same way; but somehow the insult had been wiped out by the mere act of self-assertion, and a boy kept his standing in the world as he could never have done if he had not left school when he was put back.

The Hydraulic ran alongside of the Academy, and at recess the boys had a good deal of fun with it, one way and another, sailing shingles with stones on them, and watching them go under one end of the culvert and come out of the other, or simply throwing rocks into the water. It does not seem very exciting when you tell of it, but it really was exciting; though it was not so exciting as to go down to the mills, where the Hydraulic plunged over that great wheel into the Miami. A foot-bridge crossed it that you could jump up and down on and almost make touch the water, and there were happier boys, who did not go to school, fishing there with men who had never gone. Sometimes the schoolboys ventured inside of the flour-mill and the iron-foundry, but I do not think this was often permitted; and, after all, the great thing was to rush over to the river-bank, all the boys and girls together, and play with the flutter-mills till the bell rang. The market-house was not far off, and they went there sometimes when it was not market-day, and played among the stalls; and once a girl caught her hand on a meat-hook. My boy had a vision of her hanging from it; but this was probably one of those grisly fancies that were always haunting him, and no fact at all. The bridge was close by the market-house, but for some reason or no reason the children never played in the bridge. Perhaps the toll-house man would not let them; my boy stood in dread of the toll-house man; he seemed to have such a severe way of taking the money from the teamsters.

Some of the boys were said to be the beaux of some of the girls. My boy did not know what that meant; in his own mind he could not disentangle the idea of bows from the idea of arrows; but he was in love with the girl who caught her hand on the meat-hook, and secretly suffered much on account of her. She had black eyes, and her name long seemed to him the most beautiful name for a girl; he said it to himself with flushes from his ridiculous little heart. While he was still a boy of ten he heard that she was married; and she must have been a great deal older than he. In fact he was too small a boy when he went to the Academy to remember how long he went there, and whether it was months or years; but probably it was not more than a year. He stopped going there because the teacher gave up the school to become a New Church minister; and as my boy's father and mother were New Church people, there must have been some intimacy between them and the teacher, which he did not know of. But he only stood in awe, not terror, of him; and he was not surprised when he met him many long years after, to find him a man peculiarly wise, gentle, and kind. Between the young and the old there is a vast gulf, seldom if ever bridged. The old can look backward over it, but they cannot cross it, any more than the young, who can see no thither side.

The next school my boy went to was a district school, as they called a public school in the Boy's Town. He did not begin going there without something more than his usual fear and trembling; for he had heard free schools and pay schools talked over among the boys, and sharply distinguished: in a pay school the teacher had only such powers of whipping as were given him by the parents, and they were always strictly limited; in a free school the teacher whipped as much and as often as he liked. For this reason it was much better to go to a pay school; but you had more fun at a free school, because there were more fellows; you must balance one thing against another. The boy who philosophized the matter in this way was a merry, unlucky fellow, who fully tested the advantages and disadvantages of the free-school system. He was one of the best-hearted boys in the world, and the kindest to little boys; he was always gay and always in trouble, and forever laughing, when he was not crying under that cruel rod. Sometimes he would not cry; but when he was caught in one of his frequent offences and called up before the teacher's desk in the face of the whole school, and whipped over his thinly jacketed shoulders, he would take it without wincing, and go smiling to his seat, and perhaps be called back and whipped more for smiling. He was a sort of hero with the boys on this account, but he was too kind-hearted to be proud, and mingled with the rest on equal terms. One awful day, just before school took up in the afternoon, he and another boy went for a bucket of drinking-water; it always took two boys. They were gone till long after school began, and when they came back the teacher called them up, and waited for them to arrive slowly at his desk while he drew his long, lithe rod through his left hand. They had to own that they had done wrong, and they had no excuse but the one a boy always has—they forgot. He said he must teach them not to forget, and their punishment began; surely the most hideous and depraving sight, except a hanging, that could be offered to children's eyes. One of them howled and shrieked, and leaped and danced, catching his back, his arms, his legs, as the strokes rained upon him, imploring, promising, and getting away at last with a wild effort to rub himself all over all at once. When it came the hero's turn, he bore it without a murmur, and as if his fortitude exasperated him, the teacher showered the blows more swiftly and fiercely upon him than before, till a tear or two did steal down the boy's cheek. Then he was sent to his seat, and in a few minutes he was happy with a trap for catching flies which he had contrived in his desk.

No doubt they were an unruly set of boys, and I do not suppose the teacher was a hard man, though he led the life of an executioner, and seldom passed a day without inflicting pain that a fiend might shrink from giving. My boy lived in an anguish of fear lest somehow he should come under that rod of his; but he was rather fond of the teacher, and so were all the boys. The teacher took a real interest in their studies, and if he whipped them well, he taught them well; and at most times he was kind and friendly with them. Anyway, he did not blister your hand with a ruler, as some teachers did, or make you stand bent forward from the middle, with your head hanging down, so that the blood all ran into it. Under him my boy made great advances in reading and writing, and he won some distinction in declamation; but the old difficulties with the arithmetic remained. He failed to make anything out of the parts of speech in his grammar; but one afternoon, while he sat in his stocking feet, trying to ease the chilblains which every boy used to have from his snow-soaked boots, before the days of india-rubbers, he found something in the back of his grammar which made him forget all about the pain. This was a part called Prosody, and it told how to make verses; explained the feet, the accents, the stanzas—everything that had puzzled him in his attempts to imitate the poems he had heard his father read aloud. He was amazed; he had never imagined that such a science existed, and yet here it was printed out, with each principle reduced to practice. He conceived of its reasons at the first reading, so that I suppose nature had not dealt so charily with him concerning the rules of prosody as the rules of arithmetic; and he lost no time in applying them in a poem of his own. The afternoon air was heavy with the heat that quivered visibly above the great cast-iron wood stove in the centre of the schoolroom; the boys drowsed in their seats, or hummed sleepily over their lessons; the chilblains gnawed away at the poet's feet, but heaven had opened to him, and he was rapt far from all the world of sense. The music which he had followed through those poems his father read was no longer a mystery; he had its key, its secret; he might hope to wield its charm, to lay its spell upon others. He wrote his poem, which was probably a simple, unconscious imitation of something that had pleased him in his school-reader, and carried it proudly home with him. But here he met with that sort of disappointment which more than any other dismays and baffles authorship; a difference in the point of view. His father said the verses were well made, and he sympathized with him in his delight at having found out the way to make them, though he was not so much astonished as the boy that such a science as prosody should exist. He praised the child's work, and no doubt smiled at it with the mother; but he said that the poem spoke of heaven as a place in the sky, and he wished him always to realize that heaven was a *state* and not a *place*, and that we could have it in this world as well as the next. The boy promised that he would try to realize heaven as a state; but at the bottom of his heart he despaired of getting that idea into poetry. Everybody else who had made poetry spoke of heaven as a place; they even called it a land, and put it in the sky; and he did not see how he was to do otherwise, no matter what Swedenborg said. He revered Swedenborg; he had a religious awe of the seer's lithograph portrait in a full-bottom wig which hung in the front-room, but he did not see how even Swedenborg could have helped calling heaven a place if he had been making poetry.

The next year, or the next quarter, maybe, there was a new teacher; they seem to have followed each other somewhat as people do in a dream; they were not there, and then they were there; but, however the new one came, the boys were some time in getting used to his authority. It appeared to them that several of his acts were distinctly tyrannical, and were encroachments upon rights of theirs which the other teacher, with all his severity, had respected. My boy was inspired by the common mood to write a tragedy which had the despotic behavior of the new teacher for its subject, and which was intended to be represented by the boys in the hayloft of a boy whose father had a stable without any horse in it. The tragedy was written in the measure of the "Lady of the Lake," which was the last poem my boy had heard his father reading aloud; it was very easy kind of verse. At the same time, the boys were to be dressed as Roman conspirators, and one of them was to give the teacher a petition to read, while another plunged a dagger into his vitals, and still another shouted, "Strike, Stephanos, strike!" It seemed to my boy that he had invented a situation which he had lifted almost bodily out of Goldsmith's history; and he did not feel that his lines,

"Come one, come all! This rock shall flee
From its firm base as soon as we,"

were too closely modelled upon Scott's lines,

"Come one, come all! This rock shall fly
From its firm base as soon as I."

The tragedy was never acted. There may have been some trouble about the hayloft; for the boy whose father owned the stable was to have got the use of it without his father's knowing it; and the poet found that the boys themselves scarcely entered into the spirit of his work. But after that there came a real tragedy, which most of them had part in without realizing it, and that was their persecution of a teacher until he had to give up the school. He must have come next after that usurper, but at any rate the word had been passed round, even before school took up the first morning he began, that he was to be resisted to the death. He could not have had any notion of what was in the air, for in that opening speech to the school which a new teacher always used to make, he talked to the boys in the friendliest manner, and with more sense and reason than they could feel, though I hope they felt some secret shame for the way they meant to behave. He took up some old, dry rods, which he had lying on his desk, and which he said he had found in it, and he told them he hoped never to use such a thing as a rod in that school, and never to strike any boy a blow. He broke the rods into small pieces and put them into the stove, and called the school to order for the studies before it. But the school never came to order, either then or afterwards. As soon as the teacher took his seat, the whispering and giggling, the scuffling and pushing began. The boys passed notes to the girls and held up their slates with things written on them to make the girls laugh; and they threw chewed-paper balls at one another. They asked to go out, and they stayed out as long as they pleased, and came back with an easy air, as if they had done nothing. They would not study; they did not care how much they missed in the class, and they laughed when they had to go to the foot. They made faces at the teacher and mocked him when his back was turned; they even threw paper wads at him.

It went on day after day till the school became a babel. The teacher tried reasoning, and such mild punishment as standing up in the middle of the floor, and keeping in after school. One big boy whom he stood up winked at the girls and made everybody titter; another whom he bade stay after school grabbed his hat and ran out of the room. The fellows played hookey as much as they wanted to, and did not give any excuse for being late, or for not coming at all. At last, when the teacher was driven desperate, and got in a rod (which he said he was ashamed to use, but they left him no hope of ruling them by reason), the big boys fought him, and struck back when he began to whip them. This gentle soul had not one friend among all those little savages, whom he had given no cause to hate, but only cause to love him. None of them could have told why they used him so ill, for nobody knew; only, the word had gone out that you were not to mind him, but to mock him and fight him; nobody knew where the word first came from.

Not even my boy, I grieve to say, was the poor man's friend, though he too had received only kindness from him. One day, when the teacher had set him his copy, and found him doing it badly as he came by, he gave him a slight tap on his head with his penknife, and addressed him some half-joking reproof. This fired my boy's wicked little heart with furious resentment; he gathered up his books after school, and took them home; a good many other boys had done it, and the school was dwindling. He was sent back with his books the next morning, and many other parents behaved as wisely as his. One of the leading men in the town, whose mere presence in the schoolroom sent a thrill of awe through the fellows, brought his son in after such an escapade, and told the teacher that he had just given him a sound thrashing, and he hoped the teacher would give him another. But the teacher took the hand of the snivelling wretch, and called him affectionately by name, and said they would try to get along without that, and sent him to his seat forgiven. It ought to have touched a heart of stone, but in that barbarous republic of boys there was no gratitude. Sometimes they barred the teacher out by nailing the doors and windows; and at last he gave up the school.

But even then his persecution did not end. The word went out that you were not to speak to him if you met him; and if he spoke to you, you were not to say anything back. One day he came up to my boy where he sat fishing for crawfish in the Hydraulic, with his bare legs dangling over the edge of a culvert, and, unawed by this august figure, asked him pleasantly what luck he had. The boy made no sign of seeing or hearing him, and he ignored some other kindly advances. I hope the teacher thought it merely his shyness. The boy went home and told, gleefully, how he had refused to speak to Old Manton; but here he met his reward. He was made to feel how basely rude he had been, and to tingle with a wholesome shame. There was some talk of sending him to the teacher, to ask his forgiveness; but this was given up for fear of inflicting pain where possibly none had been felt. I wish now the boy could have gone to him, for perhaps the teacher is no longer living.

VII.
MANNERS AND CUSTOMS.

I sometimes wonder how much these have changed since my boy's time. Of course they differ somewhat from generation to generation, and from East to West and North to South, but not so much, I believe, as grown people are apt to think. Everywhere and always the world of boys is outside of the laws that govern grown-up communities, and it has its unwritten usages, which are handed down from old to young, and perpetuated on the same level of years, and are lived into and lived out of, but are binding, through all personal vicissitudes, upon the great body of boys between six and twelve years old. No boy can violate them without losing his standing among the other boys, and he cannot enter into their world without coming under them. He must do this, and must not do that; he obeys, but he does not know why, any more than the far-off savages from whom his customs seem mostly to have come. His world is all in and through the world of men and women, but no man or woman can get into it any more than if it were a world of invisible beings. It has its own ideals and superstitions, and these are often of a ferocity, a depravity, scarcely credible in after-life. It is a great pity that fathers and mothers cannot penetrate that world; but they cannot, and it is only by accident that they can catch some glimpse of what goes on in it. No doubt it will be civilized in time, but it will be very slowly; and in the meanwhile it is only in some of its milder manners and customs that the boy's world can be studied.

The first great law was that, whatever happened to you through another boy, whatever hurt or harm he did you, you were to right yourself upon his person if you could; but if he was too big, and you could not hope to revenge yourself, then you were to bear the wrong, not only for that time, but for as many times as he chose to inflict it. To tell the teacher or your mother, or to betray your tormentor to any one outside of the boys' world, was to prove yourself a cry-baby, without honor or self-respect, and unfit to go with the other fellows. They would have the right to mock you, to point at you, and call "E-e-e, e-e-e, e-e-e!" at you, till you fought them. After that, whether you whipped them or not there began to be some feeling in your favor again, and they had to stop.

Every boy who came to town from somewhere else, or who moved into a new neighborhood, had to fight the old residents. There was no reason for this, except that he was a stranger, and there appeared to be no other means of making his acquaintance. If he was generally whipped he became subject to the local tribe, as the Delawares were to the Iroquois in the last century; if he whipped the other boys, then they adopted him into their tribe, and he became a leader among them. When you moved away from a neighborhood you did not lose all your rights in it; you did not have to fight when you went back to see the boys, or anything; but if one of them met you in your new precincts you might have to try conclusions with him; and perhaps, if he was a boy who had been in the habit of whipping you, you were quite ready to do so. When my boy's family left the Smith house, one of the boys from that neighborhood came up to see him at the Falconer house, and tried to carry things with a high hand, as he had always done. Then my boy fought him, quite as if he were not a Delaware and the other boy not an Iroquois, with sovereign rights over him. My boy was beaten, but the difference was that, if he had not been on new ground, he would have been beaten without daring to fight. His mother witnessed the combat, and came out and shamed him for his behavior, and had in the other boy, and made them friends over some sugar-cakes. But after that the boys of the Smith neighborhood understood that my boy would not be whipped without fighting. The home instruction was all against fighting; my boy was taught that it was not only wicked, but foolish; that if it was wrong to strike, it was just as wrong to strike back; that two wrongs never made a right, and so on. But all this was not of the least effect with a hot temper amid the trials and perplexities of life in the Boy's Town.

There were some boys of such standing as bullies and such wide fame that they could range all neighborhoods of the town not only without fear of being molested, or made to pass under the local yoke anywhere, but with such plenary powers of intimidation that the other boys submitted to them without question. My boy had always heard of one of these bullies, whose very name, Buz Simpson, carried terror with it; but he had never seen him, because he lived in the unknown region bordering on the river south of the Thomas house. One day he suddenly appeared, when my boy was playing marbles with some other fellows in front of the Falconer house, attended by two or three other boys from below the Sycamore Grove. He was small and insignificant, but such was the fear his name inspired that my boy and his friends cowered before him, though some of them were no mean fighters themselves. They seemed to know by instinct that this was Buz Simpson, and they stood patiently by while he kicked their marbles out of the ring and broke up their game, and, after staying awhile to cover them with ignominy and insult, passed on with his retainers to other fields of conquest. If it had been death to resist him, they could not have dreamed less of doing so; and though this outrage took place under my boy's own windows, and a single word would have brought efficient aid (for the mere sight of any boy's mother could put to flight a whole army of other boys), he never dreamed of calling for help.

That would have been a weakness which would not only have marked him forever as a cry-baby, but an indecorum too gross for words. It would have been as if, when once the boys were playing trip at school, and a big boy tripped him, and he lay quivering and panting on the ground, he had got up as soon as he could catch his breath and gone in and told the teacher; or as if, when the fellows were playing soak-about, and he got hit in the pit of the stomach with a hard ball, he had complained of the fellow who threw it. There were some things so base that a boy could not do them; and what happened out of doors, and strictly within the boy's world, had to be kept sacredly secret among the boys. For instance, if you had been beguiled, as a little boy, into being the last in the game of snap-the-whip, and the snap sent you rolling head over heels on the hard ground, and skinned your nose and tore your trousers, you could cry from the pain without disgrace, and some of the fellows would come up and try to comfort you; but you were bound in honor not to appeal to the teacher, and you were expected to use every device to get the blood off you before you went in, and to hide the tear in your trousers. Of course, the tear and the blood could not be kept from the anxious eyes at home, but even there you were expected not to say just what boys did it.

They were by no means the worst boys who did such things, but only the most thoughtless. Still, there was a public opinion in the Boy's Town which ruled out certain tricks, and gave the boys who played them the name of being "mean." One of these was boring a hole in the edge of your school-desk to meet a shaft sunk from the top, which you filled with slate-pencil dust. Then, if you were that kind of boy, you got some little chap to put his eye close to the shaft, with the hope of seeing Niagara Falls, and set your lips to the hole in the edge, and blew his eye full of pencil-dust. This was mean; and it was also mean to get some unsuspecting child to close the end of an elderwood tube with his thumb, and look hard at you, while you showed him Germany. You did this by pulling a string below the tube, and running a needle into his thumb. My boy discovered Germany in this way long before he had any geographical or political conception of it.

I do not know why, if these abominable cruelties were thought mean, it was held lawful to cover a stone with dust and get a boy, not in the secret, to kick the pile over with his bare foot. It was perfectly good form, also, to get a boy, if you could, to shut his eyes, and then lead him into a mud-puddle or a thicket of briers or nettles, or to fool him in any heartless way, such as promising to pump easy when he put his mouth to the pump-spout, and then coming down on the pump-handle with a rush that flooded him with water and sent him off blowing the tide from his nostrils like a whale. Perhaps these things were permitted because the sight of the victim's suffering was so funny. Half the pleasure in fighting wasps or bumble-bees was in killing them and destroying their nests; the other half was in seeing the fellows get stung. If you could fool a fellow into a mass-meeting of bumble-bees, and see him lead them off in a steeple-chase, it was right and fair to do so. But there were other cases in which deceit was not allowable. For instance, if you appeared on the playground with an apple, and all the boys came whooping round, "You know *me*, Jimmy!" "You know your uncle!" "You know your grandfather!" and you began to sell out bites at three pins for a lady-bite and six pins for a hog-bite, and a boy bought a lady-bite and then took a hog-bite, he was held in contempt, and could by no means pass it off for a good joke on you; it was considered mean.

In the Boy's Town there was almost as much stone-throwing as there was in Florence in the good old times. There was a great abundance of the finest kind of pebbles, from the size of a robin's egg upward, smooth and shapely, which the boys called rocks. They were always stoning something, birds, or dogs, or mere inanimate marks, but most of the time they were stoning one another. They came out of their houses, or front-yards, and began to throw stones, when they were on perfectly good terms, and they usually threw stones in parting for the day. They stoned a boy who left a group singly, and it was lawful for him to throw stones back at the rest, if the whim took him, when he got a little way off. With all this stone-throwing, very little harm was done, though now and then a stone took a boy on the skull, and raised a lump of its own size. Then the other boys knew, by the roar of rage and pain he set up, that he had been hit, and ran home and left him to his fate.

Their fights were mostly informal scuffles, on and off in a flash, and conducted with none of the ceremony which I have read of concerning the fights of English boys. It was believed that some of the fellows knew how to box, and all the fellows intended to learn, but nobody ever did. The fights sprang usually out of some trouble of the moment; but at times they were arranged to settle some question of moral or physical superiority. Then one boy put a chip on his shoulder and dared the other to knock it off. It took a great while to bring the champions to blows, and I have known the mere preparatory insults of a fight of this kind to wear out the spirit of the combatants and the patience of the spectators, so that not a blow was struck, finally, and the whole affair fell through.

Though they were so quarrelsome among themselves, the boys that my boy went with never molested girls. They mostly ignored them; but they would have scorned to hurt a girl almost as much as they would have scorned to play with one. Of course while they were very little they played with girls; and after they began to be big boys, eleven or twelve years old, they began to pay girls some attention; but for the rest they simply left them out of the question, except at parties, when the games obliged them to take some notice of the girls. Even then, however, it was not good form for a boy to be greatly interested in them; and he had to conceal any little fancy he had about this girl or that unless he wanted to be considered soft by the other fellows. When they were having fun they did not want to have any girls around; but in the back-yard a boy might play teeter or seesaw, or some such thing, with his sisters and their friends, without necessarily losing caste, though such things were not encouraged. On the other hand, a boy was bound to defend them against anything that he thought slighting or insulting; and you did not have to verify the fact that anything had been said or done; you merely had to hear that it had. It once fell to my boy to avenge such a reported wrong from a boy who had not many friends in school, a timid creature whom the mere accusation frightened half out of his wits, and who wildly protested his innocence. He ran, and my boy followed with the other boys after him, till they overtook the culprit and brought him to bay against a high board fence; and there my boy struck him in his imploring face. He tried to feel like a righteous champion, but he felt like a brutal ruffian. He long had the sight of that terrified, weeping face, and with shame and sickness of heart he cowered before it. It was pretty nearly the last of his fighting; and though he came off victor, he felt that he would rather be beaten himself than do another such act of justice. In fact, it seems best to be very careful how we try to do justice in this world, and mostly to leave retribution of all kinds to God, who really knows about things; and content ourselves as much as possible with mercy, whose mistakes are not so irreparable.

The boys had very little to do with the inside of one another's houses. They would follow a boy to his door, and wait for him to come out; and they would sometimes get him to go in and ask his mother for crullers or sugar-cakes; when they came to see him they never went indoors for him, but stood on the sidewalk and called him with a peculiar cry, something like "E-oo-we, e-oo-we!" and threw stones at trees, or anything, till he came out. If he did not come, after a reasonable time, they knew he was not there, or that his mother would not let him come. A fellow was kept in that way, now and then. If a fellow's mother came to the door the boys always ran.

The mother represented the family sovereignty; the father was seldom seen, and he counted for little or nothing among the outside boys. It was the mother who could say whether a boy might go fishing or in swimming, and she was held a good mother or not according as she habitually said yes or no. There was no other standard of goodness for mothers in the boy's world, and could be none; and a bad mother might be outwitted by any device that the other boys could suggest to her boy. Such a boy was always willing to listen to any suggestion, and no boy took it hard if the other fellows made fun when their plan got him into trouble at home. If a boy came out after some such experience with his face wet, and his eyes red, and his lips swollen, of course you had to laugh; he expected it, and you expected him to stone you for laughing.

When a boy's mother had company, he went and hid till the guests were gone, or only came out of concealment to get some sort of shy lunch. If the other fellows' mothers were there, he might be a little bolder, and bring out cake from the second table. But he had to be pretty careful how he conformed to any of the usages of grown-up society. A fellow who brushed his hair, and put on shoes, and came into the parlor when there was company, was not well seen among the fellows; he was regarded in some degree as a girl-boy; a boy who wished to stand well with other boys kept in the wood-shed, and only went in as far as the kitchen to get things for his guests in the back-yard. Yet there were mothers who would make a boy put on a collar when they had company, and disgrace him before the world by making him stay round and help; they acted as if they had no sense and no pity; but such mothers were rare.

Most mothers yielded to public opinion and let their boys leave the house, and wear just what they always wore. I have told how little they wore in summer. Of course in winter they had to put on more things. In those days knickerbockers were unknown, and if a boy had appeared in short pants and long stockings he would have been thought dressed like a circus-actor. Boys wore long pantaloons, like men, as soon as they put off skirts, and they wore jackets or roundabouts such as the English boys still wear at Eton. When the cold weather came they had to put on shoes and stockings, or rather long-legged boots, such as are seen now only among lumbermen and teamsters in the country. Most of the fellows had stoga boots, as heavy as iron and as hard; they were splendid to skate in, they kept your ankles so stiff. Sometimes they greased them to keep the water out; but they never blacked them except on Sunday, and before Saturday they were as red as a rusty stove-pipe. At night they were always so wet that you could not get them off without a boot-jack, and you could hardly do it anyway; sometimes you got your brother to help you off with them, and then he pulled you all round the room. In the morning they were dry, but just as hard as stone, and you had to soap the heel of your woollen sock (which your grandmother had knitted for you, or maybe some of your aunts) before you could get your foot in, and sometimes the ears of the boot that you pulled it on by would give way, and you would have to stamp your foot in and kick the toe against the mopboard. Then you gasped and limped round, with your feet like fire, till you could get out and limber your boots up in some water somewhere. About noon your chilblains began.

My boy had his secret longing to be a dandy, and once he was so taken with a little silk hat at the hat-store that he gave his father no peace till he got it for him. But the very first time he wore it the boys made fun of it, and that was enough. After that he wore it several times with streaming tears; and then he was allowed to lay it aside, and compromise on an unstylish cap of velvet, which he had despised before. I do not know why a velvet cap was despised, but it was; a cap with a tassel was babyish. The most desired kind of cap was a flat one of blue broadcloth, with a patent-leather peak, and a removable cover of oil-cloth, silk if you were rich, cotton if you were poor; when you had pulled the top of such a cap over on one side, you were dressed for conquest, especially if you wore your hair long. My boy had such a cap, with a silk oil-cloth cover, but his splendor was marred by his short hair.

At one time boots with long, sharp-pointed toes were the fashion, and he so ardently desired a pair of these that fate granted his prayer, but in the ironical spirit which fate usually shows when granting a person's prayers. These boots were of calf-skin, and they had red leather tops, which you could show by letting your pantaloon-legs carelessly catch on the ears; but the smallest pair in town was several sizes too large for my boy. The other boys were not slow to discover the fact, and his martyrdom with these boots began at once. But he was not allowed to give them up as he did the silk hat; he had to wear them out. However, it did not take long to wear out a pair of boots in the Boy's Town. A few weeks' scuffling over the gravelly ground, or a single day's steady sliding made them the subjects for half-soling, and then it was a question of only a very little time.

A good many of the boys, though, wore their boots long after they were worn out, and so they did with the rest of their clothes. I have tried to give some notion of the general distribution of comfort which was never riches in the Boy's Town; but I am afraid that I could not paint the simplicity of things there truly without being misunderstood in these days of great splendor and great squalor. Everybody had enough, but nobody had too much; the richest man in town might be worth twenty thousand dollars. There were distinctions among the grown people, and no doubt there were the social cruelties which are the modern expression of the savage spirit otherwise repressed by civilization; but these were unknown among the boys. Savages they were, but not that kind of savages. They valued a boy for his character and prowess, and it did not matter in the least that he was ragged and dirty. Their mothers might not allow him the run of their kitchens quite so freely as some other boys, but the boys went with him just the same, and they never noticed how little he was washed and dressed. The best of them had not an overcoat; and underclothing was unknown among them. When a boy had buttoned up his roundabout, and put on his mittens, and tied his comforter round his neck and over his ears, he was warmly dressed.

VIII.
PLAYS AND PASTIMES.

About the time fate cursed him with a granted prayer in those boots, my boy was deep in the reading of a book about Grecian mythology which he found perpetually fascinating; he read it over and over without ever thinking of stopping merely because he had already been through it twenty or thirty times. It had pictures of all the gods and goddesses, demigods and heroes; and he tried to make poems upon their various characters and exploits. But Apollo was his favorite, and I believe it was with some hope of employing them in a personation of the god that he coveted those red-topped sharp-toed calf-skin boots. He had a notion that if he could get up a chariot by sawing down the sides of a store-box for the body, and borrowing the hind-wheels of the baby's willow wagon, and then, drawn by the family dog Tip at a mad gallop, come suddenly whirling round the corner of the school-house, wearing spangled circus-tights and bearing Apollo's bow and shaft, while a silken scarf which he had seen in a bureau-drawer at home blew gallantly out behind him, it would have a fine effect with the boys. Some of the fellows wished to be highway robbers and outlaws; one who intended to be a pirate afterwards got so far in a maritime career as to invent a steam-engine governor now in use on the seagoing steamers; my boy was content to be simply a god, the god of poetry and sunshine. He never realized his modest ambition, but then boys never realize anything; though they have lots of fun failing.

"A CITIZEN'S CHARACTER FOR CLEVERNESS OR MEANNESS WAS FIXED BY HIS WALKING ROUND OR OVER THE RINGS."

In the Boy's Town they had regular games and plays, which came and went in a stated order. The first thing in the spring as soon as the frost began to come out of the ground, they had marbles which they played till the weather began to be pleasant for the game, and then they left it off. There were some mean-spirited fellows who played for fun, but any boy who was anything played for keeps: that is, keeping all the marbles he won. As my boy was skilful at marbles, he was able to start out in the morning with his toy, or the marble he shot with, and a commy, or a brown marble of the Lowest value, and come home at night with a pocketful of white-alleys and blood-alleys, striped plasters find bull's-eyes, and crystals, clear and clouded. His gambling was not approved of at home, but it was allowed him because of the hardness of his heart, I suppose, and because it was not thought well to keep him up too strictly; and I suspect it would have been useless to forbid his playing for keeps, though he came to have a bad conscience about it before he gave it up. There were three kinds of games at marbles which the boys played: one with a long ring marked out on the ground, and a base some distance off, which you began to shoot from; another with a round ring, whose line formed the base; and another with holes, three or five, hollowed in the earth at equal distances from each other, which was called knucks. You could play for keeps in all these games; and in knucks, if you won, you had a shot or shots at the knuckles of the fellow who lost, and who was obliged to hold them down for you to shoot at. Fellows who were mean would twitch their knuckles away when they saw your toy coming, and run; but most of them took their punishment with the savage pluck of so many little Sioux. As the game began in the raw cold of the earliest spring, every boy had chapped hands, and nearly every one had the skin worn off the knuckle of his middle finger from resting it on the ground when he shot. You could use a knuckle-dabster of fur or cloth to rest your hand on, but it was considered effeminate, and in the excitement you were apt to forget it, anyway. Marbles were always very exciting, and were played with a clamor as incessant as that of a blackbird roost. A great many points were always coming up: whether a boy took-up or edged beyond the very place where his toy lay when he shot; whether he knuckled down, or kept his hand on the ground in shooting; whether, when another boy's toy drove one marble against another and knocked both out of the ring, he holloed "Fen doubs!" before the other fellow holloed "Doubs!" whether a marble was in or out of the ring, and whether the umpire's decision was just or not. The gambling and the quarrelling went on till the second-bell rang for school, and began again as soon as the boys could get back to their rings when school let out. The rings were usually marked on the ground with a stick, but when there was a great hurry, or there was no stick handy, the side of a fellow's boot would do, and the hollows for knucks were always bored by twirling round on your boot-heel. This helped a boy to wear out his boots very rapidly, but that was what his boots were made for, just as the sidewalks were made for the boys' marble-rings, and a citizen's character for cleverness or meanness was fixed by his walking round or over the rings. Cleverness was used in the Virginia sense for amiability; a person who was clever in the English sense was smart.

There were many games of ball. Two-cornered cat was played by four boys: two to bat, and two behind the batters to catch and pitch. Three-cornered cat was, I believe, the game which has since grown into base-ball, and was even then sometimes called so. But soak-about was the favorite game at school, and it simply consisted of hitting any other boy you could with the ball when you could get it. Foot-ball was always played with a bladder, and it came in season with the cold weather when the putting up of beef began; the business was practically regarded by the boys as one undertaken to supply them with bladders for foot-balls.

When the warm weather came on in April, and the boys got off their shoes for good, there came races, in which they seemed to fly on wings. Life has a good many innocent joys for the human animal, but surely none so ecstatic as the boy feels when his bare foot first touches the breast of our mother earth in the spring. Something thrills through him then from the heart of her inmost being that makes him feel kin with her, and cousin to all her dumb children of the grass and trees. His blood leaps as wildly as at that kiss of the waters when he plunges into their arms in June; there is something even finer and sweeter in the rapture of the earlier bliss. The day will not be long enough for his flights, his races; he aches more with regret than with fatigue when he must leave the happy paths under the stars outside, and creep into his bed. It is all like some glimpse, some foretaste of the heavenly time when the earth and her sons shall be reconciled in a deathless love, and they shall not be thankless, nor she a step-mother any more.

About the only drawback to going barefoot was stumping your toe, which you were pretty sure to do when you first took off your shoes and before you had got used to your new running weight. When you struck your toe against a rock, or anything, you caught it up in your hand, and hopped about a hundred yards before you could bear to put it to the ground. Then you sat down, and held it as tight as you could, and cried over it, till the fellows helped you to the pump to wash the blood off. Then, as soon as you could, you limped home for a rag, and kept pretty quiet about it so as to get out again without letting on to your mother.

With the races came the other plays which involved running, like hide-and-go-whoop, and tag, and dog-on-wood, and horse, which I dare say the boys of other times and other wheres know by different names. The Smith-house neighborhood was a famous place for them all, both because there were such lots of boys, and because there were so many sheds and stables where you could hide, and everything. There was a town pump there for you, so that you would not have to go into the house for a drink when you got thirsty, and perhaps be set to doing something; and there were plenty of boards for teeter and see-saw; and somehow that neighborhood seemed to understand boys, and did not molest them in any way. In a vacant lot behind one of the houses there was a whirligig, that you could ride on and get sick in about a minute; it was splendid. There was a family of German boys living across the street, that you could stone whenever they came out of their front gate, for the simple and sufficient reason that they were Dutchmen, and without going to the trouble of a quarrel with them. My boy was not allowed to stone them; but when he was with the other fellows, and his elder brother was not along, he could not help stoning them.

There were shade trees all along that street, that you could climb if you wanted to, or that you could lie down under when you had run yourself out of breath, or play mumble-the-peg. My boy distinctly remembered that under one of these trees his elder brother first broached to him that awful scheme of reform about fibbing, and applied to their own lives the moral of "The Trippings of Tom Pepper;" he remembered how a conviction of the righteousness of the scheme sank into his soul, and he could not withhold his consent. Under the same tree, and very likely at the same time, a solemn conclave of boys, all the boys there were, discussed the feasibility of tying a tin can to a dog's tail, and seeing how he would act. They had all heard of the thing, but none of them had seen it; and it was not so much a question of whether you ought to do a thing that on the very face of it would be so much fun, and if it did not amuse the dog as highly as anybody, could certainly do him no harm, as it was a question of whose dog you should get to take the dog's part in the sport. It was held that an old dog would probably not keep still long enough for you to tie the can on; he would have his suspicions; or else he would not run when the can was tied on, but very likely just go and lie down somewhere. The lot finally fell to a young yellow dog belonging to one of the boys, and the owner at once ran home to get him, and easily lured him back to the other boys with flatteries and caresses. The flatteries and caresses were not needed, for a dog is always glad to go with boys, upon any pretext, and so far from thinking that he does them a favor, he feels himself greatly honored. But I dare say the boy had a guilty fear that if his dog had known why he was invited to be of that party of boys, he might have pleaded a previous engagement. As it was, he came joyfully, and allowed the can to be tied to his tail without misgiving. If there had been any question with the boys as to whether he would enter fully into the spirit of the affair, it must have been instantly dissipated by the dog's behavior when he felt the loop tighten on his tail, and looked round to see what the matter was. The boys hardly had a chance to cheer him before he flashed out of sight round the corner, and they hardly had time to think before he flashed into sight again from the other direction. He whizzed along the ground, and the can hurtled in the air, but there was no other sound, and the cheers died away on the boys' lips. The boy who owned the dog began to cry, and the other fellows began to blame him for not stopping the dog. But he might as well have tried to stop a streak of lightning; the only thing you could do was to keep out of the dog's way. As an experiment it was successful beyond the wildest dreams of its projectors, though it would have been a sort of relief if the dog had taken some other road, for variety, or had even reversed his course. But he kept on as he began, and by a common impulse the boys made up their minds to abandon the whole affair to him. They all ran home and hid, or else walked about and tried to ignore it. But at this point the grown-up people began to be interested; the mothers came to their doors to see what was the matter. Yet even the mothers were powerless in a case like that, and the enthusiast had to be left to his fate. He was found under a barn at last, breathless, almost lifeless, and he tried to bite the man who untied the can from his tail. Eventually he got well again, and lived to be a solemn warning to the boys; he was touchingly distrustful of their advances for a time, but he finally forgot and forgave everything. They did not forget, and they never tried tying a tin can to a dog's tail again, among all the things they tried and kept trying. Once was enough; and they never even liked to talk of it, the sight was so awful. They were really fond of the dog, and if they could have thought he would take the matter so seriously, they would not have tried to have that kind of fun with him. It cured them of ever wanting to have that kind of fun with any dog.

As the weather softened, tops came in some weeks after marbles went out, and just after foot-races were over, and a little before swimming began. At first the boys bought their tops at the stores, but after a while the boy whose father had the turning-shop on the Hydraulic learned to turn their tops, and did it for nothing, which was cheaper than buying tops, especially as he furnished the wood, too, and you only had to get the wire peg yourself. I believe he was the same boy who wanted to be a pirate and ended by inventing a steam-governor. He was very ingenious, and he knew how to turn a top out of beech or maple that would outspin anything you could get in a store. The boys usually chose a firm, smooth piece of sidewalk, under one of the big trees in the Smith neighborhood, and spun their tops there. A fellow launched his top into the ring, and the rest waited till it began to go to sleep, that is, to settle in one place, and straighten up and spin silently, as if standing still. Then any fellow had a right to peg at it with his top, and if he hit it, he won it; and if he split it, as sometimes happened, the fellow that owned it had to give him a top. The boys came with their pockets bulged out with tops, but before long they had to go for more tops to that boy who could turn them. From this it was but another step to go to the shop with him and look on while he turned the tops; and then in process of time the boys discovered that the smooth floor of the shop was a better place to fight tops than the best piece of sidewalk. They would have given whole Saturdays to the sport there, but when they got to holloing too loudly the boy's father would come up, and then they would all run. It was considered mean in him, but the boy himself was awfully clever, and the first thing the fellows knew they were back there again. Some few of the boys had humming-tops; but though these pleased by their noise, they were not much esteemed, and could make no head against the good old turnip-shaped tops, solid and weighty, that you could wind up with a stout cotton cord, and launch with perfect aim from the flat button held between your fore finger and middle finger. Some of the boys had a very pretty art in the twirl they gave the top, and could control its course, somewhat as a skilful pitcher can govern that of a base-ball.

I do not know why a certain play went out, but suddenly the fellows who had been playing ball, or marbles, or tops, would find themselves playing something else. Kites came in just about the time of the greatest heat in summer, and lasted a good while; but could not have lasted as long as the heat, which began about the first of June, and kept on well through September; no play could last so long as that, and I suppose kite-flying must have died into swimming after the Fourth of July. The kites were of various shapes: bow kites, two-stick kites, and house kites. A bow kite could be made with half a barrel hoop carried over the top of a cross, but it was troublesome to make, and it did not fly very well, and somehow it was thought to look babyish; but it was held in greater respect than the two-stick kite, which only the smallest boys played with, and which was made by fastening two sticks in the form of a cross. Any fellow more than six years old who appeared on the Commons with a two-stick kite would have been met with jeers, as a kind of girl. The favorite kite, the kite that balanced best, took the wind best, and flew best, and that would stand all day when you got it up, was the house kite, which was made of three sticks, and shaped nearly in the form of the gable of a gambrel-roofed house, only smaller at the base than at the point where the roof would begin. The outline of all these kites was given, and the sticks stayed in place by a string carried taut from stick to stick, which was notched at the ends to hold it; sometimes the sticks were held with a tack at the point of crossing, and sometimes they were mortised into one another; but this was apt to weaken them. The frame was laid down on a sheet of paper, and the paper was cut an inch or two larger, and then pasted and folded over the string. Most of the boys used a paste made of flour and cold water; but my boy and his brother could usually get paste from the printing-office; and when they could not they would make it by mixing flour and water cream-thick, and slowly boiling it. That was a paste that would hold till the cows came home, the boys said, and my boy was courted for his skill in making it. But after the kite was pasted, and dried in the sun, or behind the kitchen stove, if you were in very much of a hurry (and you nearly always were), it had to be hung, with belly-bands and tail-bands; that is, with strings carried from stick to stick over the face and at the bottom, to attach the cord for flying it and to fasten on the tail by. This took a good deal of art, and unless it were well done the kite would not balance, but would be always pitching and darting. Then the tail had to be of just the right weight; if it was too heavy the kite kept sinking, even after you got it up where otherwise it would stand; if too light, the kite would dart, and dash itself to pieces on the ground. A very pretty tail was made by tying twists of paper across a string a foot apart, till there were enough to balance the kite; but this sort of tail was apt to get tangled, and the best tail was made of a long streamer of cotton rags, with a gay tuft of dog-fennel at the end. Dog-fennel was added or taken away till just the right weight was got; and when this was done, after several experimental tests, the kite was laid flat on its face in the middle of the road, or on a long stretch of smooth grass; the bands were arranged, and the tail stretched carefully out behind, where it would not catch on bushes. You unwound a great length of twine, running backward, and letting the twine slip swiftly through your hands till you had run enough out; then you seized the ball, and with one look over your shoulder to see that all was right, started swiftly forward. The kite reared itself from the ground, and, swaying gracefully from side to side, rose slowly into the air, with its long tail climbing after it till the fennel tuft swung free. If there was not much surface wind you might have to run a little way, but as soon as the kite caught the upper currents it straightened itself, pulled the twine taut, and steadily mounted, while you gave it more and more twine; if the breeze was strong, the cord burned as it ran through your hands; till at last the kite stood still in the sky, at such a height that the cord holding it sometimes melted out of sight in the distance.

 If it was a hot July day the sky would be full of kites, and the Commons would be dotted over with boys holding them, or setting them up, or winding them in, and all talking and screaming at the tops of their voices under the roasting sun. One might think that kite-flying, at least, could be carried on quietly and peaceably; but it was not. Besides the wild debate of the rival excellences of the different kites, there were always quarrels from getting the strings crossed; for, as the boys got their kites up, they drew together for company and for an easier comparison of their merits. It was only a mean boy who would try to cross another fellow's string; but sometimes accidents would happen; two kites would become entangled, and both would have to be hauled in, while their owners cried and scolded, and the other fellows cheered and laughed. Now and then the tail of a kite would part midway, and then the kite would begin to dart violently from side to side, and then to whirl round and round in swifter and narrower circles till it dashed itself to the ground. Sometimes the kite-string would break, and the kite would waver and fall like a bird shot in the wing; and the owner of the kite, and all the fellows who had no kites, would run to get it where it came down, perhaps a mile or more away. It usually came down in a tree, and they had to climb for it; but sometimes it lodged so high that no one could reach it; and then it was slowly beaten and washed away in the winds and rains, and its long tail left streaming all winter from the naked bough where it had caught. It was so good for kites on the Commons, because there were no trees there, and not even fences, but a vast open stretch of level grass, which the cows and geese kept cropped to the earth; and for the most part the boys had no trouble with their kites there. Some of them had paper fringe pasted round the edges of their kites; this made a fine rattling as the kite rose, and when the kite stood, at the end of its string, you could hear the humming if you put your ear to the twine. But the most fun was sending up messengers. The messengers were cut out of thick paper, with a slit at one side, so as to slip over the string, which would be pulled level long enough to give the messenger a good start, and then released, when the wind would catch the little circle, and drive it up the long curving incline till it reached the kite.

KITE TIME.

It was thought a great thing in a kite to pull, and it was a favor to another boy to let him take hold of your string and feel how your kite pulled. If you wanted to play mumble-the-peg, or anything, while your kite was up, you tied it to a stake in the ground, or gave it to some other fellow to hold; there were always lots of fellows eager to hold it. But you had to be careful how you let a little fellow hold it; for, if it was a very powerful kite, it would take him up. It was not certain just how strong a kite had to be to take a small boy up, and nobody had ever seen a kite do it, but everybody expected to see it.

IX.
CIRCUSES AND SHOWS.
What every boy expected to do, some time or other, was to run off. He expected to do this because the scheme offered an unlimited field to the imagination, and because its

fulfilment would give him the highest distinction among the other fellows. To run off was held to be the only way for a boy to right himself against the wrongs and hardships of a boy's life. As far as the Boy's Town was concerned, no boy had anything to complain of; the boys had the best time in the world there, and in a manner they knew it. But there were certain things that they felt no boy ought to stand, and these things were sometimes put upon them at school, but usually at home. In fact, nearly all the things that a fellow intended to run off for were done to him by those who ought to have been the kindest to him. Some boys' mothers had the habit of making them stop and do something for them just when they were going away with the fellows. Others would not let them go in swimming as often as they wanted, and, if they saw them with their shirts on wrong side out, would not believe that they could get turned in climbing a fence. Others made them split kindling and carry in wood, and even saw wood. None of these things, in a simple form, was enough to make a boy run off, but they prepared his mind for it, and when complicated with whipping they were just cause for it. Weeding the garden, though, was a thing that almost, in itself, was enough to make a fellow run off.

Not many of the boys really had to saw wood, though a good many of the fellows' fathers had saws and bucks in their wood-sheds. There were public sawyers who did most of the wood-sawing; and they came up with their bucks on their shoulders, and asked for the job almost as soon as the wood was unloaded before your door. The most popular one with the boys was a poor half-wit known among them as Morn; and he was a favorite with them because he had fits, and because, when he had a fit, he would seem to fly all over the woodpile. The boys would leave anything to see Morn in a fit, and he always had a large crowd round him as soon as the cry went out that he was beginning to have one. They watched the hapless creature with grave, unpitying, yet not unfriendly interest, too ignorant of the dark ills of life to know how deeply tragic was the spectacle that entertained them, and how awfully present in Morn's contortions was the mystery of God's ways with his children, some of whom he gives to happiness and some to misery. When Morn began to pick himself weakly up, with eyes of pathetic bewilderment, they helped him find his cap, and tried to engage him in conversation, for the pleasure of seeing him twist his mouth when he said, of a famous town drunkard whom he admired, "He's a strong man; he eats liquor." It was probably poor Morn's ambition to eat liquor himself, and the boys who followed that drunkard about to plague him had a vague respect for his lamentable appetite.

None of the boys ever did run off, except the son of one of the preachers. He was a big boy, whom my boy remotely heard of, but never saw, for he lived in another part of the town; but his adventure was known to all the boys, and his heroism rated high among them. It took nothing from this, in their eyes, that he was found, homesick and crying in Cincinnati, and was glad to come back—the great fact was that he had run off; nothing could change or annul that. If he had made any mistake, it was in not running off with a circus, for that was the true way of running off. Then, if you were ever seen away from home, you were seen tumbling through a hoop and alighting on the crupper of a barebacked piebald, and if you ever came home you came home in a gilded chariot, and you flashed upon the domestic circle in flesh-colored tights and spangled breech-cloth. As soon as the circus-bills began to be put up you began to hear that certain boys were going to run off with that circus, and the morning after it left town you heard they had gone, but they always turned up at school just the same. It was believed that the circus-men would take any boy who wanted to go with them, and would fight off his friends if they tried to get him away.

The boys made a very careful study of the circus-bills, and afterwards, when the circus came, they held the performance to a strict account for any difference between the feats and their representation. For a fortnight beforehand they worked themselves up for the arrival of the circus into a fever of fear and hope, for it was always a question with a great many whether they could get their fathers to give them the money to go in. The full price was two bits, and the half-price was a bit, or a Spanish *real*, then a commoner coin than the American dime in the West; and every boy, for that time only, wished to be little enough to look young enough to go in for a bit. Editors of newspapers had a free ticket for every member of their families; and my boy was sure of going to the circus from the first rumor of its coming. But he was none the less deeply thrilled by the coming event, and he was up early on the morning of the great day, to go out and meet the circus procession beyond the corporation line.

I do not really know how boys live through the wonder and the glory of such a sight. Once there were two chariots—one held the band in red-and-blue uniforms, and was drawn by eighteen piebald horses; and the other was drawn by a troop of Shetland ponies, and carried in a vast mythical sea-shell little boys in spangled tights and little girls in the gauze skirts and wings of fairies. There was not a flaw in this splendor to the young eyes that gloated on it, and that followed it in rapture through every turn and winding of its course in the Boy's Town; nor in the magnificence of the actors and actresses, who came riding two by two in their circus-dresses after the chariots, and looking some haughty and contemptuous, and others quiet and even bored, as if it were nothing to be part of such a procession. The boys tried to make them out by the pictures and names on the bills: which was Rivers, the bare-back rider, and which was O'Dale, the champion tumbler; which was the India-rubber man, which the ring-master, which the clown. Covered with dust, gasping with the fatigue of a three hours' run beside the procession, but fresh at heart as in the beginning, they arrived with it on the Commons, where the tent-wagons were already drawn up, and the ring was made, and mighty men were driving the iron-headed tent-stakes, and stretching the ropes of the great skeleton of the pavilion which they were just going to clothe with canvas. The boys were not allowed to come anywhere near, except three or four who got leave to fetch water from a neighboring well, and thought themselves richly paid with half-price tickets. The other boys were proud to pass a word with them as they went by with their brimming buckets; fellows who had money to go in would have been glad to carry water just for the glory of coming close to the circus-men. They stood about in twos and threes, and lay upon the grass in groups debating whether a tan-bark ring was better than a sawdust ring; there were different opinions. They came as near the wagons as they dared, and looked at the circus-horses munching hay from the tail-boards, just like common horses. The wagons were left standing outside of the tent; but when it was up, the horses were taken into the dressing-room, and then the boys, with many a backward look at the wide spread of canvas, and the flags and streamers floating over it from the centre-pole (the centre-pole was revered almost like a distinguished personage), ran home to dinner so as to get back good and early, and be among the first to go in. All round, before the circus doors were open, the doorkeepers of the side-shows were inviting people to come in and see the giants and fat woman and boa-constrictors, and there were stands for peanuts and candy and lemonade; the vendors cried, "Ice-cold lemonade, from fifteen hundred miles under ground! Walk up, roll up, tumble up, any way to get up!" The boys thought this brilliant drolling, but they had no time to listen after the doors were open, and they had no money to spend on side-shows or dainties, anyway. Inside the tent, they found it dark and cool, and their hearts thumped in their throats with the wild joy of being there; they recognized one another with amaze, as if they had not met for years, and the excitement kept growing, as other fellows came in. It was lots of fun, too, watching the country-jakes, as the boys called the farmer-folk, and seeing how green they looked, and how some of them tried to act smart with the circus-men that came round with oranges to sell. But the great thing was to see whether fellows that said they were going to hook in really got in. The boys held it to be a high and creditable thing to hook into a show of any kind, but hooking into a circus was something that a fellow ought to be held in special honor for doing. He ran great risks, and if he escaped the vigilance of the massive circus-man who patrolled the outside of the tent with a cowhide and a bulldog, perhaps he merited the fame he was sure to win.

I do not know where boys get some of the notions of morality that govern them. These notions are like the sports and plays that a boy leaves off as he gets older to the boys that are younger. He outgrows them, and other boys grow into them, and then outgrow them as he did. Perhaps they come down to the boyhood of our time from the boyhood of the race, and the unwritten laws of conduct may have prevailed among the earliest Aryans on the plains of Asia that I now find so strange in a retrospect of the Boy's Town. The standard of honor there was, in a certain way, very high among the boys; they would have despised a thief as he deserved, and I cannot remember one of them who might not have been safely trusted. None of them would have taken an apple out of a market-wagon, or stolen a melon from a farmer who came to town with it; but they would all have thought it fun, if not right, to rob an orchard or hook a watermelon out of a patch. This would have been a foray into the enemy's country, and the fruit of the adventure would have been the same as the plunder of a city, or the capture of a vessel belonging to him on the high seas. In the same way, if one of the boys had seen a circus-man drop a quarter, he would have hurried to give it back to him, but he would only have been proud to hook into the circus-man's show, and the other fellows would have been proud of his exploit, too, as something that did honor to them all. As a person who enclosed bounds and forbade trespass, the circus-man constituted himself the enemy of every boy who respected himself, and challenged him to practise any sort of strategy. There was not a boy in the crowd that my boy went with who would have been allowed to hook into a circus by his parents; yet hooking in was an ideal that was cherished among them, that was talked of, and that was even sometimes attempted, though not often. Once, when a fellow really hooked in, and joined the crowd that had ignobly paid, one of the fellows could not stand it. He asked him just how and where he got in, and then he went to the door, and got back his money from the doorkeeper upon the plea that he did not feel well; and in five or ten minutes he was back among the boys, a hero of such moral grandeur as would be hard to describe. Not one of the fellows saw him as he really was—a little lying, thievish scoundrel. Not even my boy saw him so, though he had on some other point of personal honesty the most fantastic scruples.

The boys liked to be at the circus early so as to make sure of the grand entry of the performers into the ring, where they caracoled round on horseback, and gave a delicious foretaste of the wonders to come. The fellows were united in this, but upon other matters feeling varied—some liked tumbling best; some the slack-rope; some bare-back riding; some the feats of tossing knives and balls and catching them. There never was more than one ring in those days; and you were not tempted to break your neck and set your eyes forever askew, by trying to watch all the things that went on at once in two or three rings. The boys did not miss the smallest feats of any performance, and they enjoyed them every one, not equally, but fully. They had their preferences, of course, as I have hinted; and one of the most popular acts was that where a horse has been trained to misbehave, so that nobody can mount him; and after the actors have tried him, the ring-master turns to the audience, and asks if some gentleman among them wants to try it. Nobody stirs, till at last a tipsy country-jake is seen making his way down from one of the top-seats towards the ring. He can hardly walk, he is so drunk, and the clown has to help him across the ring-board, and even then he trips and rolls over on the sawdust, and has to be pulled to his feet. When they bring him up to the horse, he falls against it; and the little fellows think he will certainly get killed. But the big boys tell the little fellows to shut up and watch out. The ring-master and the clown manage to get the country-jake on to the broad platform on the horse's back, and then the ring-master cracks his whip, and the two supes who have been holding the horse's head let go, and the horse begins cantering round the ring. The little fellows are just sure the country-jake is going to fall off, he reels and totters so; but the big boys tell them to keep watching out; and pretty soon the country-jake begins to straighten up. He begins to unbutton his long gray overcoat, and then he takes it off and throws it into the ring, where one of the supes catches it. Then he sticks a short pipe into his mouth, and pulls on an old wool hat, and flourishes a stick that the supe throws to him, and you see that he is an Irishman just come across the sea; and then off goes another coat, and he comes out a British soldier in white duck trousers and red coat. That comes off, and he is an American sailor, with his hands on his hips dancing a hornpipe. Suddenly away flash wig and beard and false-face, the pantaloons are stripped off with the same movement, the actor stoops for the reins lying on the horse's neck, and James Rivers, the greatest three-horse rider in the world nimbly capers on the broad pad, and kisses his hand to the shouting and cheering spectators as he dashes from the ring past the braying and bellowing brass-band into the dressing-room!

The big boys have known all along that he was not a real country-jake; but when the trained mule begins, and shakes everybody off, just like the horse, and another country-jake gets up, and offers to bet that he can ride that mule, nobody can tell whether he is a real country-jake or not. This is always the last thing in the performance, and the boys have seen with heavy hearts many signs openly betokening the end which they knew was at hand. The actors have come out of the dressing-room door, some in their everyday clothes, and some with just overcoats on over their circus-dresses, and they lounge about near the band-stand watching the performance in the ring. Some of the people are already getting up to go out, and stand for this last act, and will not mind the shouts of "Down in front! Down there!" which the boys eagerly join in, to eke out their bliss a little longer by keeping away even the appearance of anything transitory in it. The country-jake comes stumbling awkwardly into the ring, but he is perfectly sober, and he boldly leaps astride the mule, which tries all its arts to shake him off, plunging, kicking, rearing. He sticks on, and everybody cheers him, and the owner of the mule begins to get mad and to make it do more things to shake the country-jake off. At last, with one convulsive spring, it flings him from its back, and dashes into the dressing-room, while the country-jake picks himself up and vanishes among the crowd.

A man mounted on a platform in the ring is imploring the ladies and gentlemen to keep their seats, and to buy tickets for the negro-minstrel entertainment which is to follow, but which is not included in the price of admission. The boys would like to stay, but they have not the money, and they go out clamoring over the performance, and trying to decide which was the best feat. As to which was the best actor, there is never any question; it is the clown, who showed by the way he turned a double somersault that he can do anything, and who chooses to be clown simply because he is too great a creature to enter into rivalry with the other actors.

There will be another performance in the evening, with real fights outside between the circus-men and the country-jakes, and perhaps some of the Basin rounders, but the boys do not expect to come; that would be too much. The boy's brother once stayed away in the afternoon, and went at night with one of the jour printers; but he was not able to report that the show was better than it was in the afternoon. He did not get home till nearly ten o'clock, though, and he saw the sides of the tent dropped before the people got out; that was a great thing; and what was greater yet, and reflected a kind of splendor on the boy at second hand, was that the jour printer and the clown turned out to be old friends. After the circus, the boy actually saw them standing near the centre-pole talking together; and the next day the jour showed the grease that had dripped on his coat from the candles. Otherwise the boy might have thought it was a dream, that some one he knew had talked on equal terms with the clown. The boys were always intending to stay up and see the circus go out of town, and they would have done so, but their mothers would not let them. This may have been one reason why none of them ever ran off with a circus.

As soon as a circus had been in town, the boys began to have circuses of their own, and to practise for them. Everywhere you could see boys upside down, walking on their hands or standing on them with their legs dangling over, or stayed against house walls. It was easy to stand on your head; one boy stood on his head so much that he had to have it shaved, in the brain fever that he got from standing on it; but that did not stop the other fellows. Another boy fell head downwards from a rail where he was skinning-the-cat, and nearly broke his neck, and made it so sore that it was stiff ever so long. Another boy, who was playing Samson, almost had his leg torn off by the fellows that were pulling at it with a hook; and he did have the leg of his pantaloons torn off. Nothing could stop the boys but time, or some other play coming in; and circuses lasted a good while. Some of the boys learned to turn hand-springs; anybody could turn cart-wheels; one fellow, across the river, could just run along and throw a somersault and light on his feet; lots of fellows could light on their backs; but if you had a spring-board, or shavings under a bank, like those by the turning-shop, you could practise for somersaults pretty safely.

All the time you were practising you were forming your circus company. The great trouble was not that any boy minded paying five or ten pins to come in, but that so many fellows wanted to belong there were hardly any left to form an audience. You could get girls, but even as spectators girls were a little *too* despicable; they did not know anything; they had no sense; if a follow got hurt they cried. Then another thing was, where to have the circus. Of course it was simply hopeless to think of a tent, and a boy's circus was very glad to get a barn. The boy whose father owned the barn had to get it for the circus without his father knowing it; and just as likely as not his mother would hear the noise and come out and break the whole thing up while you were in the very middle of it. Then there were all sorts of anxieties and perplexities about the dress. You could do something by turning your roundabout inside out, and rolling your trousers up as far as they would go; but what a fellow wanted to make him a real circus actor was a long pair of white cotton stockings, and I never knew a fellow that got a pair; I heard of many a fellow who was said to have got a pair; but when you came down to the fact, they vanished like ghosts when you try to verify them. I believe the fellows always expected to get them out of a bureau-drawer or the clothes-line at home, but failed. In most other ways, a boy's circus was always a failure, like most other things boys undertake. They usually broke up under the strain of rivalry; everybody wanted to be the clown or ring-master; or else the boy they got the barn of behaved badly, and went into the house crying, and all the fellows had to run.

There were only two kinds of show known by that name in the Boy's Town: a Nigger Show, or a performance of burnt-cork minstrels; and an Animal Show, or a strolling menagerie; and the boys always meant a menagerie when they spoke of a show, unless they said just what sort of show. The only perfect joy on earth in the way of an entertainment, of course, was a circus, but after the circus the show came unquestionably next. It made a processional entry into the town almost as impressive as the circus's, and the boys went out to meet it beyond the corporation line in the same way. It always had two elephants, at least, and four or five camels, and sometimes there was a giraffe. These headed the procession, the elephants in the very front, with their keepers at their heads, and then the camels led by halters dangling from their sneering lips and contemptuous noses. After these began to come the show-wagons, with pictures on their sides, very flattered portraits of the wild beasts and birds inside; lions first, then tigers (never meaner than Royal Bengal ones, which the boys understood to be a superior breed), then leopards, then pumas and panthers; then bears, then jackals and hyenas; then bears and wolves; then kangaroos, musk-oxen, deer, and such harmless cattle; and then ostriches, emus, lyre-birds, birds-of-Paradise and all the rest. From time to time the boys ran back from the elephants and camels to get what good they could out of the scenes in which these hidden wonders were dramatized in acts of rapine or the chase, but they always came forward to the elephants and camels again. Even with them they had to endure a degree of denial, for although you could see most of the camels' figures, the elephants were so heavily draped that it was a kind of disappointment to look at them. The boys kept as close as they could, and came as near getting under the elephants' feet as the keepers would allow; but, after all, they were driven off a good deal and had to keep stealing back. They gave the elephants apples and bits of cracker and cake, and some tried to put tobacco into their trunks; though they knew very well that it was nearly certain death to do so; for any elephant that was deceived that way would recognize the boy that did it, and kill him the next time he came, if it was twenty years afterwards. The boys used to believe that the Miami bridge would break down under the elephants if they tried to cross it, and they would have liked to see it do it, but no one ever saw it, perhaps because the elephants always waded the river. Some boys had seen them wading it, and stopping to drink and squirt the water out of their trunks. If an elephant got a boy that had given him tobacco into the river, he would squirt water on him till he drowned him. Still, some boys always tried to give the elephants tobacco, just to see how they would act for the time being.

A show was not so much in favor as a circus, because there was so little performance in the ring. You could go round and look at the animals, mostly very sleepy in their cages, but you were not allowed to poke them through the bars, or anything; and when you took your seat there was nothing much till Herr Driesbach entered the lions' cage, and began to make them jump over his whip. It was some pleasure to see him put his head between the jaws of the great African King of Beasts, but the lion never did anything to him, and so the act wanted a true dramatic climax. The boys would really rather have seen a bare-back rider, like James Rivers, turn a back-somersault and light on his horse's crupper, any time, though they respected Herr Driesbach, too; they did not care much for a woman who once went into the lions' cage and made them jump round.

If you had the courage you could go up the ladder into the curtained tower on the elephant's back, and ride round the ring with some of the other fellows; but my boy at least never had the courage; and he never was of those who mounted the trick pony and were shaken off as soon as they got on. It seemed to be a good deal of fun, but he did not dare to risk it; and he had an obscure trouble of mind when, the last thing, four or five ponies were brought out with as many monkeys tied on their backs, and set to run a race round the ring. The monkeys always looked very miserable, and even the one who won the race, and rode round afterwards with an American flag in his hand and his cap very much cocked over his left eye, did not seem to cheer up any.

The boys had their own beliefs about the different animals, and one of these concerned the inappeasable ferocity of the zebra. I do not know why the zebra should have had this repute, for he certainly never did anything to deserve it; but, for the matter of that, he was like all the other animals. Bears were not much esteemed, but they would have been if they could have been really seen hugging anybody to death. It was always hoped that some of the fiercest animals would get away and have to be hunted down, and retaken after they had killed a lot of dogs. If the elephants, some of them, had gone crazy, it would have been something, for then they would have roamed up and down the turnpike smashing buggies and wagons, and had to be shot with the six-pound cannon that was used to celebrate the Fourth of July with.

Another thing that was against the show was that the animals were fed after it was out, and you could not see the tigers tearing their prey when the great lumps of beef were thrown them. There was somehow not so much chance of hooking into a show as a circus, because the seats did not go all round, and you could be seen under the cages as soon as you got in under the canvas. I never heard of a boy that hooked into a show; perhaps nobody ever tried.

A show had the same kind of smell as a circus, up to a certain point, and then its smell began to be different. Both smelt of tan-bark or saw-dust and trodden grass, and both smelt of lemonade and cigars; but after that a show had its own smell of animals. I have found in later life that this is a very offensive smell on a hot day; but I do not believe a boy ever thinks so; for him it is just a different smell from a circus smell. There were two other reasons why a show was not as much fun as a circus, and one was that it was thought instructive, and fellows went who were not allowed to go to circuses. But the great reason of all was that you could not have an animal show of your own as you could a circus. You could not get the animals; and no boy living could act a camel, or a Royal Bengal tiger, or an elephant so as to look the least like one.

Of course you could have negro shows, and the boys often had them; but they were not much fun, and you were always getting the black on your shirt-sleeves.

THE CIRCUS.

X.
HIGHDAYS AND HOLIDAYS.

"THE BOYS BEGAN TO CELEBRATE IT WITH GUNS AND PISTOLS."

The greatest day of all in the Boy's Town was Christmas. In that part of the West the boys had never even heard of Thanksgiving, and their elders knew of it only as a festival of far-off New England. Christmas was the day that was kept in all churches and families, whether they were Methodists or Episcopalians, Baptists or Universalists, Catholics or Protestants; and among boys of whatever persuasion it was kept in a fashion that I suppose may have survived from the early pioneer times, when the means of expressing joy were few and primitive. On Christmas eve, before the church-bells began to ring in the day, the boys began to celebrate it with guns and pistols, with shooting-crackers and torpedoes; and they never stopped as long as their ammunition lasted. A fellow hardly ever had more than a bit to spend, and after he had paid ten cents for a pack of crackers, he had only two cents and a half for powder; and if he wanted his pleasure to last, he had to be careful. Of course he wanted his pleasure to last, but he would rather have had no pleasure at all than be careful, and most of the boys woke Christmas morning empty-handed, unless they had burst their pistols the night before; then they had a little powder left, and could go pretty well into the forenoon if they could find some other boy who had shot off his powder but had a whole pistol left. Lots of fellows' pistols got out of order without bursting, and that saved powder; but generally a fellow kept putting in bigger and bigger loads till his pistol blew to pieces. There were all sorts of pistols; but the commonest was one that the boys called a Christmas-crack; it was of brass, and when it burst the barrel curled up like a dandelion stem when you split it and put it in water. A Christmas-crack in that shape was a trophy; but of course the little boys did not have pistols; they had to put up with shooting-crackers, or maybe just torpedoes. Even then the big boys would get to fire them off on one pretext or another. Some fellows would hold a cracker in their hands till it exploded; nearly everybody had burned thumbs, and some of the boys had their faces blackened with powder. Now and then a fellow who was nearly grown up would set off a whole pack of crackers in a barrel; it seemed almost incredible to the little boys.

It was glorious, and I do not think any of the boys felt that there was anything out of keeping in their way of celebrating the day, for I do not think they knew why they were celebrating it, or, if they knew, they never thought. It was simply a holiday, and was to be treated like a holiday. After all, perhaps there are just as strange things done by grown people in honor of the loving and lowly Saviour of Men; but we will not enter upon that question. When they had burst their pistols or fired off their crackers, the boys sometimes huddled into the back part of the Catholic church and watched the service, awed by the dim altar lights, the rising smoke of incense, and the grimness of the sacristan, an old German, who stood near to keep order among them. They knew the fellows who were helping the priest; one of them was the boy who stood on his head till he had to have it shaved; they would have liked to mock him then and there for wearing a petticoat, and most of them had the bitterest scorn and hate for Catholics in their hearts; but they were afraid of the sacristan, and they behaved very well as long as they were in the church; but as soon as they got out they whooped and yelled, and stoned the sacristan when he ran after them.

My boy would have liked to do all that too, just to be with the crowd, but at home he had been taught to believe that Catholics were as good as anybody, and that you must respect everybody's religion. His father and the priest were friendly acquaintances, and in a dim way he knew that his father had sometimes taken the Catholics' part in his paper when the prejudice against foreigners ran high. He liked to go to the Catholic church, though he was afraid of the painted figure that hung full length on the wooden crucifix, with the blood-drops under the thorns on its forehead, and the red wound in its side. He was afraid of it as something both dead and alive; he could not keep his eyes away from the awful, beautiful, suffering face, and the body that seemed to twist in agony, and the hands and feet so cruelly nailed to the cross.

But he never connected the thought of that anguish with Christmas. His head was too full of St. Nicholas, who came down the chimney, and filled your stockings; the day belonged to St. Nicholas. The first thing when you woke you tried to catch everybody, and you caught a person if you said "Christmas Gift!" before he or she did; and then the person you caught had to give you a present. Nobody ever said "Merry Christmas!" as people do now; and I do not know where the custom of saying "Christmas Gift" came from. It seems more sordid and greedy than it really was; the pleasure was to see who could say it first; and the boys did not care for what they got if they beat, any more than they cared for what they won in fighting eggs at Easter.

At New-Year's the great thing was to sit up and watch the old year out; but the little boys could not have kept awake even if their mothers had let them. In some families, perhaps of Dutch origin, the day was kept instead of Christmas, but for most of the fellows it was a dull time. You had spent all your money at Christmas, and very likely burst your pistol, anyway. It was some consolation to be out of school, which did not keep on New-Year's; and if it was cold you could have fires on the ice; or, anyway, you could have fires on the river-bank, or down by the shore, where there was always plenty of drift-wood.

But New-Year's could not begin to compare with Easter. All the boys' mothers colored eggs for them at Easter; I do not believe there was a mother in the Boy's Town mean enough not to. By Easter Day, in that Southern region, the new grass was well started, and grass gave a beautiful yellow color to the eggs boiled with it. Onions colored them a soft, pale green, and logwood, black; but the most esteemed egg of all was a calico-egg. You got a piece of new calico from your mother, or maybe some of your aunts, and you got somebody (most likely your grandmother, if she was on a visit at the time) to sew an egg up in it; and when the egg was boiled it came out all over the pattern of the calico. My boy's brother once had a calico-egg that seemed to my boy a more beautiful piece of color than any Titian he has seen since; it was kept in a bureau-drawer till nobody could stand the smell. But most Easter eggs never outlasted Easter Day. As soon as the fellows were done breakfast they ran out of the house and began to fight eggs with the other fellows. They struck the little ends of the eggs together, and if your egg broke another fellow's egg, then you had a right to it. Sometimes an egg was so hard that it would break every other egg in the street; and generally when a little fellow lost his egg, he began to cry and went into the house. This did not prove him a cry-baby; it was allowable, like crying when you stumped your toe. I think this custom of fighting eggs came from the Pennsylvania Germans, to whom the Boy's Town probably owed its Protestant observance of Easter. There was nothing religious in the way the boys kept it, any more than there was in their way of keeping Christmas.

I do not think they distinguished between it and All-Fool's Day in character or dignity. About the best thing you could do then was to write April Fool on a piece of paper and pin it to a fellow's back, or maybe a girl's, if she was a big girl, and stuck-up, or anything. I do not suppose there is a boy now living who is silly enough to play this trick on anybody, or mean enough to fill an old hat with rocks and brickbats, and dare a fellow to kick it; but in the Boy's Town there were some boys who did this; and then the fellow had to kick the hat, or else come under the shame of having taken a dare. Most of the April-foolings were harmless enough, like saying, "Oh, see that flock of wild-geese flying over!" and "What have you got on the back of your coat!" and holloing "April Fool!" as soon as the person did it. Sometimes a crowd of boys got a bit with a hole in it, and tied a string in it, and laid it on the sidewalk, and then hid in a cellar, and when anybody stooped to pick it up, they pulled it in. That was the greatest fun, especially if the person was stingy; but the difficulty was to get the bit, whether it had a hole in it or not.

From the first of April till the first of May was a long stretch of days, and you never heard any one talk about a May Party till April Fool was over. Then there always began to be talk of a May Party, and who was going to be invited. It was the big girls that always intended to have it, and it was understood at once who was going to be the Queen. At least the boys had no question, for there was one girl in every school whom all the boys felt to be the most beautiful; but probably there was a good deal of rivalry and heart-burning among the girls themselves. Very likely it was this that kept a May Party from hardly ever coming to anything but the talk. Besides the Queen, there were certain little girls who were to be Lambs; I think there were Maids of Honor, too; but I am not sure. The Lambs had to keep very close to the Queen's person, and to wait upon her; and there were boys who had to hold the tassels of the banners which the big boys carried. These boys had to wear white pantaloons, and shoes and stockings, and very likely gloves, and to suffer the jeers of the other fellows who were not in the procession. The May Party was a girl's affair altogether, though the boys were expected to help; and so there were distinctions made that the boys never dreamed of in their rude republic, where one fellow was as good as another, and the lowest-down boy in town could make himself master if he was bold and strong enough. The boys did not understand those distinctions, and nothing of them remained in their minds after the moment; but the girls understood them, and probably they were taught at home to feel the difference between themselves and other girls, and to believe themselves of finer clay. At any rate, the May Party was apt to be poisoned at its source by questions of class; and I think it might have been in the talk about precedence, and who should be what, that my boy first heard that such and such a girl's father was a mechanic, and that it was somehow dishonorable to be a mechanic. He did not know why, and he has never since known why, but the girls then knew why, and the women seem to know now. He was asked to be one of the boys who held the banner-tassels, and he felt this a great compliment somehow, though he was so young that he had afterwards only the vaguest remembrance of marching in the procession, and going to a raw and chilly grove somewhere, and having untimely lemonade and cake. Yet these might have been the associations of some wholly different occasion.

No aristocratic reserves marred the glory of Fourth of July. My boy was quite a well-grown boy before he noticed that there were ever any clouds in the sky except when it was going to rain. At all other times, especially in summer, it seemed to him that the sky was perfectly blue, from horizon to horizon; and it certainly was so on the Fourth of July. He usually got up pretty early, and began firing off torpedoes and shooting-crackers, just as at Christmas. Everybody in town had been wakened by the salutes fired from the six-pounder on the river-bank, and by the noise of guns and pistols; and right after breakfast you heard that the Butler Guards were out, and you ran up to the court-house yard with the other fellows to see if it was true. It was not true, just yet, perhaps, but it came true during the forenoon, and in the meantime the court-house yard was a scene of festive preparation. There was going to be an oration and a public dinner, and they were already setting the tables under the locust-trees. There may have been some charge for this dinner, but the boys never knew of that, or had any question of the bounty that seemed free as the air of the summer day.

High Street was thronged with people, mostly country-jakes who had come to town with their wagons and buggies for the celebration. The young fellows and their girls were walking along hand in hand, eating gingerbread, and here and there a farmer had already begun his spree, and was whooping up and down the sidewalk unmolested by authority. The boys did not think it at all out of the way for him to be in that state; they took it as they took the preparations for the public dinner, and no sense of the shame and sorrow it meant penetrated their tough ignorance of life. He interested them because, after the regular town drunkards, he was a novelty; but, otherwise, he did not move them. By and by they would see him taken charge of by his friends and more or less brought under control; though if you had the time to follow him up you could see him wanting to fight his friends and trying to get away from them. Whiskey was freely made and sold and drunk in that time and that region; but it must not be imagined that there was no struggle against intemperance. The boys did not know it, but there was a very strenuous fight in the community against the drunkenness that was so frequent; and there were perhaps more people who were wholly abstinent then than there are now. The forces of good and evil were more openly arrayed against each other among people whose passions were strong and still somewhat primitive; and those who touched not, tasted not, handled not, far outnumbered those who looked upon the wine when it was red. The pity for the boys was that they saw the drunkards every day, and the temperance men only now and then; and out of the group of boys who were my boy's friends, many kindly fellows came to know how strong drink could rage, how it could bite like the serpent, and sting like an adder.

But the temperance men made a show on the Fourth of July as well as the drunkards, and the Sons of Temperance walked in the procession with the Masons and the Odd-Fellows. Sometimes they got hold of a whole Fourth, and then there was nothing but a temperance picnic in the Sycamore Grove, which the boys took part in as Sunday-school scholars. It was not gay; there was no good reason why it should leave the boys with the feeling of having been cheated out of their holiday, but it did. A boy's Fourth of July seemed to end about four o'clock, anyhow. After that, he began to feel gloomy, no matter what sort of a time he had. That was the way he felt after almost any holiday.

Market-day was a highday in the Boy's Town, and it would be hard to say whether it was more so in summer than in winter. In summer, the market opened about four or five o'clock in the morning, and by this hour my boy's father was off twice a week with his market-basket on his arm. All the people did their marketing in the same way; but it was a surprise for my boy, when he became old enough to go once with his father, to find the other boys' fathers at market too. He held on by his father's hand, and ran by his side past the lines of wagons that stretched sometimes from the bridge to the court-house, in the dim morning light. The market-house, where the German butchers in their white aprons were standing behind their meat-blocks, was lit up with candles in sconces, that shone upon festoons of sausage and cuts of steak dangling from the hooks behind them; but without, all was in a vague obscurity, broken only by the lanterns in the farmers' wagons. There was a market-master, who rang a bell to open the market, and if anybody bought or sold anything before the tap of that bell, he would be fined. People would walk along the line of wagons, where the butter and eggs, apples and peaches and melons, were piled up inside near the tail-boards, and stop where they saw something they wanted, and stand near so as to lay hands on it the moment the bell rang. My boy remembered stopping that morning by the wagon of some nice old Quaker ladies, who used to come to his house, and whom his father stood chatting with till the bell rang. They probably had an understanding with him about the rolls of fragrant butter which he instantly lifted into his basket. But if you came long after the bell rang, you had to take what you could get.

There was a smell of cantaloupes in the air, along the line of wagons, that morning, and so it must have been towards the end of the summer. After the nights began to lengthen and to be too cold for the farmers to sleep in their wagons, as they did in summer on the market eves, the market time was changed to midday. Then it was fun to count the wagons on both sides of the street clear to where they frayed off into wood-wagons, and to see the great heaps of apples and cabbages, and potatoes and turnips, and all the other fruits and vegetables which abounded in that fertile country. There was a great variety of poultry for sale, and from time to time the air would be startled with the clamor of fowls transferred from the coops where they had been softly crr-crring in soliloquy to the hand of a purchaser who walked off with them and patiently waited for their well-grounded alarm to die away. All the time the market-master was making his rounds; and if he saw a pound roll of butter that he thought was under weight, he would weigh it with his steelyards, and if it was too light he would seize it. My boy once saw a confiscation of this sort with such terror as he would now, perhaps, witness an execution.

XI.
MUSTERS AND ELECTIONS.

The Butler Guards were the finest military company in the world. I do not believe there was a fellow in the Boy's Town who ever even tried to imagine a more splendid body of troops: when they talked of them, as they did a great deal, it was simply to revel in the recognition of their perfection. I forget just what their uniform was, but there were white pantaloons in it, and a tuft of white-and-red cockerel plumes that almost covered the front of the hat, and swayed when the soldier walked, and blew in the wind. I think the coat was gray, and the skirts were buttoned back with buff, but I will not be sure of this; and somehow I cannot say how the officers differed from the privates in dress; it was impossible for them to be more magnificent. They walked backwards in front of the platoons, with their swords drawn, and held in their white-gloved hands at hilt and point, and kept holloing, "Shoulder-r-r—arms! Carry—arms! Present—arms!" and then faced round, and walked a few steps forward, till they could think of something else to make the soldiers do.

THE "BUTLER GUARDS."

Every boy intended to belong to the Butler Guards when he grew up; and he would have given anything to be the drummer or the marker. These were both boys, and they were just as much dressed up as the Guards themselves, only they had caps instead of hats with plumes. It was strange that the other fellows somehow did not know who these boys were; but they never knew, or at least my boy never knew. They thought more of the marker than of the drummer; for the marker carried a little flag, and when the officers holloed out, "By the left flank—left! Wheel!" he set his flag against his shoulder, and stood marking time with his feet till the soldiers all got by him, and then he ran up to the front rank, with the flag fluttering behind him. The fellows used to wonder how he got to be marker, and to plan how they could get to be markers in other companies, if not in the Butler Guards. There were other companies that used to come to town on the Fourth of July and Muster Day, from smaller places round about; and some of them had richer uniforms: one company had blue coats with gold epaulets, and gold braid going down in loops on the sides of their legs; all the soldiers, of course, had braid straight down the outer seams of their pantaloons. One Muster Day, a captain of one of the country companies came home with my boy's father to dinner; he was in full uniform, and he put his plumed helmet down on the entry table just like any other hat.

There was a company of Germans, or Dutchmen, as the boys always called them; and the boys believed that they each had hay in his right shoe, and straw in his left, because a Dutchman was too dumb, as the boys said for stupid, to know his feet apart any other way; and that the Dutch officers had to call out to the men when they were marching, "Up mit de hay-foot, down mit de straw-foot—*links, links, links!*" (Left, left, left!) But the boys honored even these imperfect intelligences so much in their quality of soldiers that they would any of them have been proud to be marker in the Dutch company; and they followed the Dutchmen round in their march as fondly as any other body of troops. Of course, school let out when there was a regular muster, and the boys gave the whole day to it; but I do not know just when the Muster Day came. They fired the cannon a good deal on the river-bank, and they must have camped somewhere near the town, though no recollection of tents remained in my boy's mind. He believed with the rest of the boys that the right way to fire the cannon was to get it so hot you need not touch it off, but just keep your thumb on the touch-hole, and take it away when you wanted the cannon to go off. Once he saw the soldiers ram the piece full of dog-fennel on top of the usual charge, and then he expected the cannon to burst. But it only roared away as usual.

The boys had their own ideas of what that cannon could do if aptly fired into a force of British, or Bridish, as they called them. They wished there could be a war with England, just to see; and their national feeling was kept hot by the presence of veterans of the War of 1812 at all the celebrations. One of the boys had a grandfather who had been in the Revolutionary War, and when he died the Butler Guards fired a salute over his grave. It was secret sorrow and sometimes open shame to my boy that his grandfather should be an Englishman, and that even his father should have been a year old when he came to this country; but on his mother's side he could boast a grandfather and a great-grandfather who had taken part, however briefly or obscurely, in both the wars against Great Britain. He hated just as much as any of the boys, or perhaps more, to be the Bridish when they were playing war, and he longed as truly as any of them to march against the hereditary, or half-hereditary, enemy.

Playing war was one of the regular plays, and the sides were always Americans and Bridish, and the Bridish always got whipped. But this was a different thing, and a far less serious thing, than having a company. The boys began to have companies after every muster, of course; but sometimes they began to have them for no external reason. Very likely they would start having a company from just finding a rooster's tail-feather, and begin making plumes at once. It was easy to make a plume: you picked up a lot of feathers that the hens and geese had dropped; and you whittled a pine stick, and bound the feathers in spirals around it with white thread. That was a first-rate plume, but the uniform offered the same difficulties as the circus dress, and you could not do anything towards it by rolling up your pantaloons. It was pretty easy to make swords out of laths, but guns again were hard to realize. Some fellows had little toy guns left over from Christmas, but they were considered rather babyish, and any kind of stick was better; the right kind of a gun for a boy's company was a wooden gun, such as some of the big boys had, with the barrel painted different from the stock. The little fellows never had any such guns, and if the question of uniform could have been got over, this question of arms would still have remained. In these troubles the fellows' mothers had to suffer almost as much as the fellows themselves, the fellows teased them so much for bits of finery that they thought they could turn to account in eking out a uniform. Once it came to quite a lot of fellows getting their mothers to ask their fathers if they would buy them some little soldier-hats that one of the hatters had laid in, perhaps after a muster, when he knew the boys would begin recruiting. My boy was by when his mother asked his father, and stood with his heart in his mouth, while the question was argued; it was decided against him, both because his father hated the tomfoolery of the thing, and because he would not have the child honor any semblance of soldiering, even such a feeble image of it as a boys' company could present. But, after all, a paper chapeau, with a panache of slitted paper, was no bad soldier-hat; it went far to constitute a whole uniform; and it was this that the boys devolved upon at last. It was the only company they ever really got together, for everybody wanted to be captain and lieutenant, just as they wanted to be clown and ring-master in a circus. I cannot understand how my boy came to hold either office; perhaps the fellows found that the only way to keep the company together was to take turn-about; but, at any rate, he was marshalling his forces near his grandfather's gate one evening when his grandfather came home to tea. The old Methodist class-leader, who had been born and brought up a Quaker, stared at the poor little apparition in horror. Then he caught the paper chapeau from the boy's head, and, saying "Dear me! Dear me!" trampled it under foot. It was an awful moment, and in his hot and bitter heart the boy, who was put to shame before all his fellows, did not know whether to order them to attack his grandfather in a body, or to engage him in single combat with his own lath-sword. In the end he did neither; his grandfather walked on into tea, and the boy was left with a wound that was sore till he grew old enough to know how true and brave a man his grandfather was in a cause where so many warlike hearts wanted courage.

It was already the time of the Mexican war, when that part of the West at least was crazed with a dream of the conquest which was to carry slavery wherever the flag of freedom went. The volunteers were mustered in at the Boy's Town; and the boys, who understood that they were real soldiers, and were going to a war where they might get killed, suffered a disappointment from the plain blue of their uniform and the simplicity of their caps, which had not the sign of a feather in them. It was a consolation to know that they were going to fight the Mexicans; not so much consolation as if it had been the Bridish, though still something. The boys were proud of them, and they did not realize that most of these poor fellows were just country-jakes. Somehow they effaced even the Butler Guards in their fancy, though the Guards paraded with them, in all their splendor, as escort.

But this civic satisfaction was alloyed for my boy by the consciousness that both his father and his grandfather abhorred the war that the volunteers were going to. His grandfather, as an Abolitionist, and his father, as a Henry Clay Whig, had both been opposed to the annexation of Texas (which the boy heard talked of without knowing in the least what annexation meant), and they were both of the mind that the war growing out of it was wanton and wicked. His father wrote against it in every number of his paper, and made himself hated among its friends, who were the large majority in the Boy's Town. My boy could not help feeling that his father was little better than a Mexican, and whilst his filial love was hurt by things that he heard to his disadvantage, he was not sure that he was not rightly hated. It gave him a trouble of mind that was not wholly appeased by some pieces of poetry that he used to hear his father reading and quoting at that time, with huge enjoyment. The pieces were called "The Biglow Papers," and his father read them out of a Boston newspaper, and thought them the wisest and wittiest things that ever were. The boy always remembered how he recited the lines—

"Ez fur war, I call it murder—
There ye hev it plain and flat;
'N I don't want to go no furder
Then my Testament fur that.
God hez said so plump and fairly:

It's as long as it is broad;
And ye'll hev to git up airly,
Ef ye want to take in God."

He thought this fine, too, but still, it seemed to him, in the narrow little world where a child dwells, that his father and his grandfather were about the only people there were who did not wish the Mexicans whipped, and he felt secretly guilty for them before the other boys.

It was all the harder to bear because, up to this time, there had been no shadow of difference about politics between him and the boys he went with. They were Whig boys, and nearly all the fellows in the Boy's Town seemed to be Whigs. There must have been some Locofoco boys, of course, for my boy and his friends used to advance, on their side, the position that

"Democrats
Eat dead rats!"

The counter-argument that
"Whigs
Eat dead pigs!"

had no force in a pork-raising country like that; but it was urged, and there must have been Democratic boys to urge it. Still, they must have been few in number, or else my boy did not know them. At any rate, they had no club, and the Whig boys always had a club. They had a Henry Clay Club in 1844, and they had Buckeye Clubs whenever there was an election for governor, and they had clubs at every exciting town or county or district election. The business of a Whig club among the boys was to raise ash flag-poles, in honor of Henry Clay's home at Ashland, and to learn the Whig songs and go about singing them. You had to have a wagon, too, and some of the club pulled while the others rode; it could be such a wagon as you went walnutting with; and you had to wear strands of buckeyes round your neck. Then you were a real Whig boy, and you had a right to throw fire-balls and roll tar-barrels for the bonfires on election nights.

I do not know why there should have been so many empty tar-barrels in the Boy's Town, or what they used so much tar for; but there were barrels enough to celebrate all the Whig victories that the boys ever heard of, and more, too; the boys did not always wait for the victories, but celebrated every election with bonfires, in the faith that it would turn out right.

Maybe the boys nowadays do not throw fire-balls, or know about them. They were made of cotton rags wound tight and sewed, and then soaked in turpentine. When a ball was lighted a boy caught it quickly up, and threw it, and it made a splendid streaming blaze through the air, and a thrilling whir as it flew. A boy had to be very nimble not to get burned, and a great many boys dropped the ball for every boy that threw it. I am not ready to say why these fire-balls did not set the Boy's Town on fire, and burn it down, but I know they never did. There was no law against them, and the boys were never disturbed in throwing them, any more than they were in building bonfires; and this shows, as much as anything, what a glorious town that was for boys. The way they used to build their bonfires was to set one tar-barrel on top of another, as high as the biggest boy could reach, and then drop a match into them; in a moment a dusky, smoky flame would burst from the top, and fly there like a crimson flag, while all the boys leaped and danced round it, and hurrahed for the Whig candidates. Sometimes they would tumble the blazing barrels over, and roll them up and down the street.

The reason why they wore buckeyes was that the buckeye was the emblem of Ohio, and Ohio, they knew, was a Whig state. I doubt if they knew that the local elections always went heavily against the Whigs; but perhaps they would not have cared. What they felt was a high public spirit, which had to express itself in some way. One night, out of pure zeal for the common good, they wished to mob the negro quarter of the town, because the "Dumb Negro" (a deaf-mute of color who was a very prominent personage in their eyes) was said to have hit a white boy. I believe the mob never came to anything. I only know that my boy ran a long way with the other fellows, and, when he gave out, had to come home alone through the dark, and was so afraid of ghosts that he would have been glad of the company of the lowest-down black boy in town.

There were always fights on election-day between well-known Whig and Democratic champions, which the boys somehow felt were as entirely for their entertainment as the circuses. My boy never had the heart to look on, but he shared the excitement of the affair, and rejoiced in the triumph of Whig principles in these contests as cordially as the hardiest witness. The fighting must have come from the drinking, which began as soon as the polls were opened, and went on all day and night with a devotion to principle which is now rarely seen. In fact, the politics of the Boy's Town seem to have been transacted with an eye single to the diversion of the boys; or if not that quite, they were marked by traits of a primitive civilization among the men. The traditions of a rude hospitality in the pioneer times still lingered, and once there was a Whig barbecue, which had all the profusion of a civic feast in mediæval Italy. Every Whig family contributed loaves of bread and boiled hams; the Whig farmers brought in barrels of cider and wagon-loads of apples; there were heaps of pies and cakes; sheep were roasted whole, and young roast pigs, with oranges in their mouths, stood in the act of chasing one another over the long tables which were spread in one of the largest pork-houses, where every comer was freely welcome. I suppose boys, though, were not allowed at the dinner; all that my boy saw of the barbecue were the heaps of loaves and hams left over, that piled the floor in one of the rooms to the ceiling.

He remained an ardent Whig till his eleventh year, when his father left the party because the Whigs had nominated, as their candidate for president, General Taylor, who had won his distinction in the Mexican war, and was believed to be a friend of slavery, though afterwards he turned out otherwise. My boy then joined a Free-Soil club, and sang songs in support of Van Buren and Adams. His faith in the purity of the Whigs had been much shaken by their behavior in trying to make capital out of a war they condemned; and he had been bitterly disappointed by their preferring Taylor to Tom Corwin, the favorite of the anti-slavery Whigs. The "Biglow Papers" and their humor might not have moved him from his life-long allegiance, but the eloquence of Corwin's famous speech against the Mexican war had grounded him in principles which he could not afterwards forsake. He had spoken passages of that speech at school; he had warned our invading hosts of the vengeance that has waited upon the lust of conquest in all times, and has driven the conquerors back with trailing battle-flags. "So shall it be with yours!" he had declaimed. "You may carry them to the loftiest peaks of the Cordilleras; they may float in insolent triumph in the halls of Montezuma; but the weakest hand in Mexico, uplifted in prayer, can call down a power against you before which the iron hearts of your warriors shall be turned into ashes!" It must have been a terrible wrench for him to part from the Whig boys in politics, and the wrench must have been a sudden one at last; he was ashamed of his father for opposing the war, and then, all at once, he was proud of him for it, and was roaring out songs against Taylor as the hero of that war, and praising Little Van, whom he had hitherto despised as the "Fox of Kinderhook."

The fox was the emblem (*totem*) of the Democrats in the campaigns of 1840 and 1844; and in their processions they always had a fox chained to the hickory flag-poles which they carried round on their wagons, together with a cock, reconciled probably in a common terror. The Whigs always had the best processions; and one of the most signal days of my boy's life was the day he spent in following round a Henry Clay procession, where the different trades and industries were represented in the wagons. There were coopers, hatters, shoemakers, blacksmiths, bakers, tinners, and others, all hard at work; and from time to time they threw out to the crowd something they had made. My boy caught a tin cup, and if it had been of solid silver he could not have felt it a greater prize. He ran home to show it and leave it in safe-keeping, and then hurried back, so as to walk with the other boys abreast of a great platform on wheels, where an old woman sat spinning inside of a log-cabin, and a pioneer in a hunting-shirt stood at the door, with his long rifle in his hand. In the window sat a raccoon, which was the Whig emblem, and which, on all their banners, was painted with the legend, "That same old Coon!" to show that they had not changed at all since the great days when they elected the pioneer, General Harrison, president of the United States. Another proof of the fact was the barrel of hard-cider which lay under the cabin window.

XII.
PETS.

As there are no longer any Whig boys in the world, the coon can no longer be kept anywhere as a political emblem, I dare say. Even in my boy's time the boys kept coons just for the pleasure of it, and without meaning to elect Whig governors and presidents with them. I do not know how they got them—they traded for them, perhaps, with fellows in the country that had caught them, or perhaps their fathers bought them in market; some people thought they were very good to eat, and, like poultry and other things for the table, they may have been brought alive to market. But, anyhow, when a boy had a coon, he had to have a store-box turned open side down to keep it in, behind the house; and he had to have a little door in the box to pull the coon out through when he wanted to show it to other boys, or to look at it himself, which he did forty or fifty times a day, when he first got it. He had to have a small collar for the coon, and a little chain, because the coon would gnaw through a string in a minute. The coon himself never seemed to take much interest in keeping a coon, or to see much fun or sense in it. He liked to stay inside his box, where he had a bed of hay, and whenever the boy pulled him out, he did his best to bite the boy. He had no tricks; his temper was bad; and there was nothing about him except the rings round his tail and his political principles that anybody could care for. He never did anything but bite, and try to get away, or else run back into his box, which smelt, pretty soon, like an animal-show; he would not even let a fellow see him eat.

My boy's brother had a coon, which he kept a good while, at a time when there was no election, for the mere satisfaction of keeping a coon. During his captivity the coon bit his keeper repeatedly through the thumb, and upon the whole seemed to prefer him to any other food; I do not really know what coons eat in a wild state, but this captive coon tasted the blood of nearly that whole family of children. Besides biting and getting away, he never did the slightest thing worth remembering; as there was no election, he did not even take part in a Whig procession. He got away two or three times. The first thing his owner would know when he pulled the chain out was that there was no coon at the end of it, and then he would have to poke round the inside of the box pretty carefully with a stick, so as not to get bitten; after that he would have to see which tree the coon had gone up. It was usually the tall locust-tree in front of the house, and in about half a second all the boys in town would be there, telling the owner of the coon how to get him. Of course the only way was to climb for the coon, which would be out at the point of a high and slender limb, and would bite you awfully, even if the limb did not break under you, while the boys kept whooping and yelling and holloing out what to do, and Tip the dog just howled with excitement. I do not know how that coon was ever caught, but I know that the last time he got away he was not found during the day, but after nightfall he was discovered by moonlight in the locust-tree. His owner climbed for him, but the coon kept shifting about, and getting higher and higher, and at last he had to be left till morning. In the morning he was not there, nor anywhere.

It had been expected, perhaps, that Tip would watch him, and grab him if he came down, and Tip would have done it probably if he had kept awake. He was a dog of the greatest courage, and he was especially fond of hunting. He had been bitten oftener by that coon than anybody but the coon's owner, but he did not care for biting. He was always getting bitten by rats, but he was the greatest dog for rats that there almost ever was. The boys hunted rats with him at night, when they came out of the stables that backed down to the Hydraulic, for water; and a dog who liked above all things to lie asleep on the back-step, by day, and would no more think of chasing a pig out of the garden than he would think of sitting up all night with a coon, would get frantic about rats, and would perfectly wear himself out hunting them on land and in the water, and keep on after the boys themselves were tired. He was so fond of hunting, anyway, that the sight of a gun would drive him about crazy; he would lick the barrel all over, and wag his tail so hard that it would lift his hind-legs off the ground.

I do not know how he came into that family, but I believe he was given to it full grown by somebody. It was some time after my boy failed to buy what he called a Confoundland dog, from a colored boy who had it for sale, a pretty puppy with white and black spots which he had quite set his heart on; but Tip more than consoled him. Tip was of no particular breed, and he had no personal beauty; he was of the color of a mouse of an elephant, and his tail was without the smallest grace; it was smooth and round, but it was so strong that he could pull a boy all over the town by it, and usually did; and he had the best, and kindest, and truest ugly old face in the world. He loved the whole human race, and as a watch-dog he was a failure through his trustful nature; he would no more have bitten a person than he would have bitten a pig; but where other dogs were concerned, he was a lion. He might be lying fast asleep in the back-yard, and he usually was, but if a dog passed the front of the house under a wagon, he would be up and after that dog before you knew what you were about. He seemed to want to fight country dogs the worst, but any strange dog would do. A good half the time he would come off best; but, however he came off, he returned to the back-yard with his tongue hanging out, and wagging his tail in good-humor with all the world. Nothing could stop him, however, where strange dogs were concerned. He was a Whig dog, of course, as any one could tell by his name, which was Tippecanoe in full, and was given him because it was the nickname of General Harrison, the great Whig who won the battle of Tippecanoe. The boys' Henry Clay Club used him to pull the little wagon that they went about in singing Whig songs, and he would pull five or six boys, guided simply by a stick which he held in his mouth, and which a boy held on either side of him. But if he caught sight of a dog that he did not know, he would drop that stick and start for that dog as far off as he could see him, spilling the Henry Clay Club out of the wagon piecemeal as he went, and never stopping till he mixed up the strange dog in a fight where it would have been hard to tell which was either champion and which was the club wagon. When the fight was over Tip would come smilingly back to the fragments of the Henry Clay Club, with pieces of the vehicle sticking about him, and profess himself, in a dog's way, ready to go on with the concert.

Any crowd of boys could get Tip to go off with them, in swimming, or hunting, or simply running races. He was known through the whole town, and beloved for his many endearing qualities of heart. As to his mind, it was perhaps not much to brag of, and he certainly had some defects of character. He was incurably lazy, and his laziness grew upon him as he grew older, till hardly anything but the sight of a gun or a bone would move him. He lost his interest in politics, and, though there is no reason to suppose that he ever became indifferent to his principles, it is certain that he no longer showed his early ardor. He joined the Free-Soil movement in 1848, and supported Van Buren and

Adams, but without the zeal he had shown for Henry Clay. Once a year as long as the family lived in the Boy's Town, the children were anxious about Tip when the dog-law was put in force, and the constables went round shooting all the dogs that were found running at large without muzzles. At this time, when Tip was in danger of going mad and biting people, he showed a most unseasonable activity, and could hardly be kept in bounds. A dog whose sole delight at other moments was to bask in the summer sun, or dream by the winter fire, would now rouse himself to an interest in everything that was going on in the dangerous world, and make forays into it at all unguarded points. The only thing to do was to muzzle him, and this was done by my boy's brother with a piece of heavy twine, in such a manner as to interfere with Tip's happiness as little as possible. It was a muzzle that need not be removed for either eating, drinking, or fighting; but it satisfied the law, and Tip always came safely through the dog-days, perhaps by favor or affection with the officers who were so inexorable with some dogs.

My boy long remembered with horror and remorse his part in giving up to justice an unconscious offender, and seeing him pay for his transgression with his life. The boy was playing before his door, when a constable came by with his rifle on his shoulder, and asked him if he had seen any unmuzzled dogs about; and partly from pride at being addressed by a constable, partly from a nervous fear of refusing to answer, and partly from a childish curiosity to see what would happen, he said, "Yes; one over there by the pork-house." The constable whistled, and the poor little animal, which had got lost from the farmer it had followed to town, came running into sight round the corner of the pork-house, and sat up on its haunches to look about. It was a small red dog, the size of a fox, and the boy always saw it afterwards as it sat there in the gray afternoon, and fascinated him with its deadly peril. The constable swung his rifle quickly to his shoulder; the sharp, whiplike report came, and the dog dropped over, and its heart's blood flowed upon the ground and lay there in a pool. The boy ran into the house, with that picture forever printed in his memory. For him it was as if he had seen a fellow-being slain, and had helped to bring him to his death.

Whilst Tip was still in his prime the family of children was further enriched by the possession of a goat; but this did not belong to the whole family, or it was, at least nominally, the property of that eldest brother they all looked up to. I do not know how they came by the goat, any more than I know how they came by Tip; I only know that there came a time when it was already in the family, and that before it was got rid of it was a presence there was no mistaking. Nobody who has not kept a goat can have any notion of how many different kinds of mischief a goat can get into, without seeming to try, either, but merely by following the impulses of its own goatishness. This one was a nanny-goat, and it answered to the name of Nanny with an intelligence that was otherwise wholly employed in making trouble. It went up and down stairs, from cellar to garret, and in and out of all the rooms, like anybody, with a faint, cynical indifference in the glance of its cold gray eyes that gave no hint of its purposes or performances. In the chambers it chewed the sheets and pillow-cases on the beds, and in the dining-room, if it found nothing else, it would do its best to eat the table-cloth. Washing-day was a perfect feast for it, for then it would banquet on the shirt-sleeves and stockings that dangled from the clothes-line, and simply glut itself with the family linen and cotton. In default of these dainties, Nanny would gladly eat a chip-hat; she was not proud; she would eat a split-basket, if there was nothing else at hand. Once she got up on the kitchen-table, and had a perfect orgy with a lot of fresh-baked pumpkin-pies she found there; she cleaned all the pumpkin so neatly out of the pastry shells that, if there had been any more pumpkin left, they could have been filled up again, and nobody could have told the difference. The grandmother, who was visiting in the house at the time, declared to the mother that it would serve the father and the boys just right if she did fill these very shells up and give them to the father and the boys to eat. But I believe this was not done, and it was only suggested in a moment of awful exasperation, and because it was the father who was to blame for letting the boys keep the goat. The mother was always saying that the goat should not stay in the house another day, but she had not the heart to insist on its banishment, the children were so fond of it. I do not know why they were fond of it, for it never showed them the least affection, but was always taking the most unfair advantages of them, and it would butt them over whenever it got the chance. It would try to butt them into the well when they leaned down to pull up the bucket from the curb; and if it came out of the house, and saw a boy cracking nuts at the low flat stone the children had in the back-yard to crack nuts on, it would pretend that the boy was making motions to insult it, and before he knew what he was about it would fly at him and send him spinning head over heels. It was not of the least use in the world, and could not be, but the children were allowed to keep it till, one fatal day, when the mother had a number of other ladies to tea, as the fashion used to be in small towns, when they sat down to a comfortable gossip over dainty dishes of stewed chicken, hot biscuit, peach-preserves, sweet tomato-pickles, and pound-cake. That day they all laid off their bonnets on the hall-table, and the goat, after demurely waiting and watching with its faded eyes, which saw everything and seemed to see nothing, discerned a golden opportunity, and began to make such a supper of bonnet-ribbons as perhaps never fell to a goat's lot in life before. It was detected in its stolen joys just as it had chewed the ribbon of a best bonnet up to the bonnet, and was chased into the back-yard; but, as it had swallowed the ribbon without being able to swallow the bonnet, it carried that with it. The boy who specially owned the goat ran it down in a frenzy of horror and apprehension, and managed to unravel the ribbon from its throat, and get back the bonnet. Then he took the bonnet in and laid it carefully down on the table again, and decided that it would be best not to say anything about the affair. But such a thing as that could not be kept. The goat was known at once to have done the mischief; and this time it was really sent away. All the children mourned it, and the boy who owned it the most used to go to the house of the people who took it, and who had a high board fence round their yard, and try to catch sight of it through the cracks. When he called "Nanny" it answered him instantly with a plaintive "Baa!" and then, after a vain interchange of lamentations, he had to come away, and console himself as he could with the pets that were left him.

    Among these were a family of white rabbits, which the boys kept in a little hutch at the bottom of the yard. They were of no more use than the goat was, but they were at least not mischievous, and there was only one of them that would bite, and he would not bite if you would take him up close behind the ears, so that he could not get at you. The rest were very good-natured, and would let you smooth them, or put them inside of your shirt-bosom, or anything. They would eat cabbage or bread or apples out of your hand; and it was fun to see their noses twitch. Otherwise they had no accomplishments. All you could do with them was to trade with other boys, or else keep the dogs from them; it was pretty exciting to keep the dogs from them. Tip was such a good dog that he never dreamed of touching the rabbits.

    Of course these boys kept chickens. The favorite chicken in those days was a small white bantam, and the more feathers it had down its legs the better. My boy had a bantam hen that was perfectly white, and so tame that she would run up to him whenever he came into the yard, and follow him round like a dog. When she had chickens she taught them to be just as fond of him, and the tiny little balls of yellow down tumbled fearlessly about in his hands, and pecked the crumbs of bread between his fingers. As they got older they ran with their mother to meet him, and when he sat down on the grass they clambered over him and crept into his shirt-bosom, and crooned softly, as they did when their mother hovered them. The boy loved them better than anything he ever had; he always saw them safe in the coop at night, and he ran out early in the morning to see how they had got through the night, and to feed them. One fatal morning he found them all scattered dead upon the grass, the mother and every one of her pretty chicks, with no sign upon them of how they had been killed. He could only guess that they had fallen a prey to rats, or to some owl that had got into their coop; but, as they had not been torn or carried away, he guessed in vain. He buried them with the sympathy of all the children and all the fellows at school who heard about the affair. It was a real grief; it was long before he could think of his loss without tears; and I am not sure there is so much difference of quality in our bereavements; the loss can hurt more or it can hurt less, but the pang must be always the same in kind.

Besides his goat, my boy's brother kept pigeons, which, again, were like the goat and the rabbits in not being of very much use. They had to be much more carefully looked after than chickens when they were young, they were so helpless in their nests, such mere weak wads of featherless flesh. At first you had to open their bills and poke the food in; and you had to look out how you gave them water for fear you would drown them; but when they got a little larger they would drink and eat from your mouth; and that was some pleasure, for they did not seem to know you from an old pigeon when you took your mouth full of corn or water and fed them. Afterwards, when they began to fly, it was a good deal of fun to keep them, and make more cots for them, and build them nests in the cots.

But they were not very intelligent pets; hardly more intelligent than the fish that the boys kept in the large wooden hogshead of rain-water at the corner of the house. They had caught some of these fish when they were quite small, and the fish grew very fast, for there was plenty of food for them in the mosquito-tadpoles that abounded in the hogshead. Then, the boys fed them every day with bread-crumbs and worms. There was one big sunfish that was not afraid of anything; if you held a worm just over him he would jump out of the water and snatch it. Besides the fish, there was a turtle in the hogshead, and he had a broad chip that he liked to sun himself on. It was fun to watch him resting on this chip, with his nose barely poked out of his shell, and his eyes, with the skin dropped over them, just showing. He had some tricks: he would snap at a stick if you teased him with it, and would let you lift him up by it. That was a good deal of pleasure.

But all these were trifling joys, except maybe Tip and Nanny, compared with the pony which the boys owned in common, and which was the greatest thing that ever came into their lives. I cannot tell just how their father came to buy it for them, or where he got it; but I dare say he thought they were about old enough for a pony, and might as well have one. It was a Mexican pony, and as it appeared on the scene just after the Mexican war, some volunteer may have brought it home. One volunteer brought home a Mexican dog, that was smooth and hairless, with a skin like an elephant, and that was always shivering round with the cold; he was not otherwise a remarkable dog, and I do not know that he ever felt even the warmth of friendship among the boys; his manners were reserved and his temper seemed doubtful. But the pony never had any trouble with the climate of Southern Ohio (which is indeed hot enough to fry a salamander in summer); and though his temper was no better than other ponies', he was perfectly approachable. I mean that he was approachable from the side, for it was not well to get where he could bite you or kick you. He was of a bright sorrel color, and he had a brand on one haunch. My boy had an ideal of a pony, conceived from pictures in his reading-books at school, that held its head high and arched its neck, and he strove by means of checks and martingales to make this real pony conform to the illustrations. But it was of no use; the real pony held his neck straight out like a ewe, or, if reined up, like a camel, and he hung his big head at the end of it with no regard whatever for the ideal. His caparison was another mortification and failure. What the boy wanted was an English saddle, embroidered on the morocco seat in crimson silk, and furnished with shining steel stirrups. What he had was the framework of a Mexican saddle, covered with rawhide, and cushioned with a blanket; the stirrups were Mexican too, and clumsily fashioned out of wood. The boys were always talking about getting their father to get them a pad, but they never did it, and they managed as they could with the saddle they had. For the most part they preferred to ride the pony barebacked, for then they could ride him double, and when they first got him they all wanted to ride him so much that they had to ride him double. They kept him going the whole day long; but after a while they calmed down enough to take him one at a time, and to let him have a chance for his meals.

They had no regular stable, and the father left the boys to fit part of the cow-shed up for the pony, which they did by throwing part of the hen-coop open into it. The pigeon-cots were just over his head, and he never could have complained of being lonesome. At first everybody wanted to feed him as well as ride him, and if he had been allowed time for it he might have eaten himself to death, or if he had not always tried to bite you or kick you when you came in with his corn. After a while the boys got so they forgot him, and nobody wanted to go out and feed the pony, especially after dark; but he knew how to take care of himself, and when he had eaten up everything there was in the cow-shed he would break out and eat up everything there was in the yard.

The boys got lots of good out of him. When you were once on his back you were pretty safe, for he was so lazy that he would not think of running away, and there was no danger unless he bounced you off when he trotted; he had a hard trot. The boys wanted to ride him standing up, like circus-actors, and the pony did not mind, but the boys could not stay on, though they practised a good deal, turn about, when the other fellows were riding their horses, standing up, on the Commons. He was not of much more use in Indian fights, for he could seldom be lashed into a gallop, and a pony that proposed to walk through an Indian fight was ridiculous. Still, with the help of imagination, my boy employed him in some scenes of wild Arab life, and hurled the Moorish javelin from him in mid-career, when the pony was flying along at the mad pace of a canal-boat. The pony early gave the boys to understand that they could get very little out of him in the way of herding the family cow. He would let them ride him to the pasture, and he would keep up with the cow on the way home, when she walked, but if they wanted anything more than that they must get some other pony. They tried to use him in carrying papers, but the subscribers objected to having him ridden up to their front doors over the sidewalk, and they had to give it up.

When he became an old story, and there was no competition for him among the brothers, my boy sometimes took him into the woods, and rode him in the wandering bridle-paths, with a thrilling sense of adventure. He did not like to be alone there, and he oftener had the company of a boy who was learning the trade in his father's printing-office. This boy was just between him and his elder brother in age, and he was the good comrade of both; all the family loved him, and made him one of them, and my boy was fond of him because they had some tastes in common that were not very common among the other boys. They liked the same books, and they both began to write historical romances. My boy's romance was founded on facts of the Conquest of Granada, which he had read of again and again in Washington Irving, with a passionate pity for the Moors, and yet with pride in the grave and noble Spaniards. He would have given almost anything to be a Spaniard, and he lived in a dream of some day sallying out upon the Vega before Granada, in silk and steel, with an Arabian charger under him that champed its bit. In the meantime he did what he could with the family pony, and he had long rides in the woods with the other boy, who used to get his father's horse when he was not using it on Sunday, and race with him through the dangling wild grape-vines and pawpaw thickets, and over the reedy levels of the river, their hearts both bounding with the same high hopes of a world that could never come true.

XIII.
GUNS AND GUNNING.

All round the Boy's Town stood the forest, with the trees that must have been well grown when Mad Anthony Wayne drove the Indians from their shadow forever. The white people had hewn space for their streets and houses, for their fields and farmsteads, out of the woods, but where the woods had been left they were of immemorial age. They were not very dense, and the timber was not very heavy; the trees stood more like trees in a park than trees in a forest; there was little or no undergrowth, except here and there a pawpaw thicket; and there were sometimes grassy spaces between them, where the may-apples pitched their pretty tents in the spring. Perhaps, at no very great distance of time, it had been a prairie country, with those wide savannahs of waving grass that took the eyes of the first-comers in the Ohio wilderness with an image of Nature long tamed to the hand of man. But this is merely my conjecture, and what I know does not bear me out in it; for the wall of forest that enclosed the Boy's Town was without a break except where the axe had made it. At some points it was nearer and at some farther; but, nearer or farther, the forest encompassed the town, and it called the boys born within its circuit, as the sea calls the boys born by its shore, with mysterious, alluring voices, kindling the blood, taking the soul with love for its strangeness. There was not a boy in the Boy's Town who would not gladly have turned from the town and lived in the woods if his mother had let him; and in every vague plan of running off the forest had its place as a city of refuge from pursuit and recapture. The pioneer days were still so close to those times that the love of solitary adventure which took the boys' fathers into the sylvan wastes of the great West might well have burned in the boys' hearts; and if their ideal of life was the free life of the woods, no doubt it was because their near ancestors had lived it. At any rate, that was their ideal, and they were always talking among themselves of how they would go farther West when they grew up, and be trappers and hunters. I do not remember any boy but one who meant to be a sailor; they lived too hopelessly far from the sea; and I dare say the boy who invented the marine-engine governor, and who wished to be a pirate, would just as soon have been a bandit of the Osage. In those days Oregon had just been opened to settlers, and the boys all wanted to go and live in Oregon, where you could stand in your door and shoot deer and wild turkey, while a salmon big enough to pull you in was tugging away at the line you had set in the river that ran before the log-cabin.

"ALL AT ONCE THERE THE INDIANS WERE."

If they could, the boys would rather have been Indians than anything else, but, as there was really no hope of this whatever, they were willing to be settlers, and fight the Indians. They had rather a mixed mind about them in the meantime, but perhaps they were not unlike other idolaters in both fearing and adoring their idols; perhaps they came pretty near being Indians in that, and certainly they came nearer than they knew. When they played war, and the war was between the whites and the Indians, it was almost as low a thing to be white as it was to be British when there were Americans on the other side; in either case you had to be beaten. The boys lived in the desire, if not the hope, of some time seeing an Indian, and they made the most of the Indians in the circus, whom they knew to be just white men dressed up; but none of them dreamed that what really happened one day could ever happen. This was at the arrival of several canal-boat loads of genuine Indians from the Wyandot Reservation in the northwestern part of the state, on their way to new lands beyond the Mississippi. The boys' fathers must have known that these Indians were coming, but it just shows how stupid the most of fathers are, that they never told the boys about it. All at once there the Indians were, as if the canal-boats had dropped with them out of heaven. There they were, crowding the decks, in their blankets and moccasins, braves and squaws and pappooses, standing about or squatting in groups, not saying anything, and looking exactly like the pictures. The squaws had the pappooses on their backs, and the men and boys had bows and arrows in their hands; and as soon as the boats landed the Indians, all except the squaws and pappooses, came ashore, and went up to the court-house yard, and began to shoot with their bows and arrows. It almost made the boys crazy.

Of course they would have liked to have the Indians shoot at birds, or some game, but they were mighty glad to have them shoot at cents and bits and quarters that anybody could stick up in the ground. The Indians would all shoot at the mark till some one hit it, and the one who hit it had the money, whatever it was. The boys ran and brought back the arrows; and they were so proud to do this that I wonder they lived through it. My boy was too bashful to bring the Indians their arrows; he could only stand apart and long to approach the filthy savages, whom he revered; to have touched the border of one of their blankets would have been too much. Some of them were rather handsome, and two or three of the Indian boys were so pretty that the Boy's Town boys said they were girls. They were of all ages, from old, withered men to children of six or seven, but they were all alike grave and unsmiling; the old men were not a whit more dignified than the children, and the children did not enter into their sport with more zeal and ardor than the wrinkled sages who shared it. In fact they were, old and young alike, savages, and the boys who looked on and envied them were savages in their ideal of a world where people spent their lives in hunting and fishing and ranging the woods, and never grew up into the toils and cares that can alone make men of boys. They wished to escape these, as many foolish persons do among civilized nations, and they thought if they could only escape them they would be happy; they did not know that they would be merely savage, and that the great difference between a savage and a civilized man is work. They would all have been willing to follow these Indians away into the far West, where they were going, and be barbarians for the rest of their days; and the wonder is that some of the fellows did not try it. After the red men had flitted away like red leaves their memory remained with the boys, and a plague of bows and arrows raged among them, and it was a good while before they calmed down to their old desire of having a gun.

But they came back to that at last, for that was the normal desire of every boy in the Boy's Town who was not a girl-boy, and there were mighty few girl-boys there. Up to a certain point, a pistol would do, especially if you had bullet-moulds, and could run bullets to shoot out of it; only your mother would be sure to see you running them, and just as likely as not would be so scared that she would say you must not shoot bullets. Then you would have to use buckshot, if you could get them anywhere near the right size, or small marbles; but a pistol was always a makeshift, and you never could hit anything with it, not even a board fence; it always kicked, or burst, or something. Very few boys ever came to have a gun, though they all expected to have one. But seven or eight boys would go hunting with one shot-gun, and take turn-about shooting; some of the little fellows never got to shoot at all, but they could run and see whether the big boys had hit anything when they fired, and that was something. This was my boy's privilege for a long time before he had a gun of his own, and he went patiently with his elder brother, and never expected to fire the gun, except, perhaps, to shoot the load off before they got back to town; they were not allowed to bring the gun home loaded. It was a gun that was pretty safe for anything in front of it, but you never could tell what it was going to do. It began by being simply an old gun-barrel, which my boy's brother bought of another boy who was sick of it for a fip, as the half-real piece was called, and it went on till it got a lock from one gunsmith and a stock from another, and was a complete gun. But this took time; perhaps a month; for the gunsmiths would only work at it in their leisure; they were delinquent subscribers, and they did it in part pay for their papers. When they got through with it my boy's brother made himself a ramrod out of a straight piece of hickory, or at least as straight as the gun-barrel, which was rather sway-backed, and had a little twist to one side, so that one of the jour printers said it was a first-rate gun to shoot round a corner with. Then he made himself a powder-flask out of an ox-horn that he got and boiled till it was soft (it smelt the whole house up), and then scraped thin with a piece of glass; it hung at his side; and he carried his shot in his pantaloons pocket. He went hunting with this gun for a good many years, but he had never shot anything with it, when his uncle gave him a smoothbore rifle, and he in turn gave his gun to my boy, who must then have been nearly ten years old. It seemed to him that he was quite old enough to have a gun; but he was mortified the very next morning after he got it by a citizen who thought differently. He had risen at daybreak to go out and shoot kildees on the Common, and he was hurrying along with his gun on his shoulder when the citizen stopped him and asked him what he was going to do with that gun. He said to shoot kildees, and he added that it was his gun. This seemed to surprise the citizen even more than the boy could have wished. He asked him if he did not think he was a pretty small boy to have a gun; and he took the gun from him, and examined it thoughtfully, and then handed it back to the boy, who felt himself getting smaller all the time. The man went his way without saying anything more, but his behavior was somehow so sarcastic that the boy had no pleasure in his sport that morning; partly, perhaps, because he found no kildees to shoot at on the Common. He only fired off his gun once or twice at a fence, and then he sneaked home with it through alleys and by-ways, and whenever he met a person he hurried by for fear the person would find him too small to have a gun.

Afterwards he came to have a bolder spirit about it, and he went hunting with it a good deal. It was a very curious kind of gun; you had to snap a good many caps on it, sometimes, before the load would go off; and sometimes it would hang fire, and then seem to recollect itself, and go off, maybe, just when you were going to take it down from your shoulder. The barrel was so crooked that it could not shoot straight, but this was not the only reason why the boy never hit anything with it. He could not shut his left eye and keep his right eye open; so he had to take aim with both eyes, or else with the left eye, which was worse yet, till one day when he was playing shinny (or hockey) at school, and got a blow over his left eye from a shinny-stick. At first he thought his eye was put out; he could not see for the blood that poured into it from the cut above it. He ran homeward wild with fear, but on the way he stopped at a pump to wash away the blood, and then he found his eye was safe. It suddenly came into his mind to try if he could not shut that eye now, and keep the right one open. He found that he could do it perfectly; by help of his handkerchief, he stanched his wound, and made himself presentable, with the glassy pool before the pump for a mirror, and went joyfully back to school. He kept trying his left eye, to make sure it had not lost its new-found art, and as soon as school was out he hurried home to share the joyful news with his family. He went hunting the very next Saturday, and at the first shot he killed a bird. It was a suicidal sap-sucker, which had suffered him to steal upon it so close that it could not escape even the vagaries of that wandering gun-barrel, and was blown into such small pieces that the boy could bring only a few feathers of it away. In the evening, when his father came home, he showed him these trophies of the chase, and boasted of his exploit with the minutest detail. His father asked him whether he had expected to eat this sap-sucker, if he could have got enough of it together. He said no, sap-suckers were not good to eat. "Then you took its poor little life merely for the pleasure of killing it," said the father. "Was it a great pleasure to see it die?" The boy hung his head in shame and silence; it seemed to him that he would never go hunting again. Of course he did go hunting often afterwards, but his brother and he kept faithfully to the rule of never killing anything that they did not want to eat. To be sure, they gave themselves a wide range; they were willing to eat almost anything that they could shoot, even blackbirds, which were so abundant and so easy to shoot. But there were some things which they would have thought it not only wanton but wicked to kill, like turtle-doves, which they somehow believed were sacred, because they were the symbols of the Holy Ghost; it was quite their own notion to hold them sacred. They would not kill robins either, because robins were hallowed by poetry, and they kept about the house, and were almost tame, so that it seemed a shame to shoot them. They were very plentiful, and so were the turtle-doves, which used to light on the basin-bank, and pick up the grain scattered there from the boats and wagons. One of the apprentices in the printing-office kept a shot-gun loaded beside the press while he was rolling, and whenever he caught the soft twitter that the doves make with their wings, he rushed out with his gun and knocked over two or three of them. He was a good shot, and could nearly always get them in range. When he brought them back, it seemed to my boy that he had committed the unpardonable sin, and that something awful would surely happen to him. But he just kept on rolling the forms of type and exchanging insults with the pressman; and at the first faint twitter of doves' wings he would be off again.

My boy and his brother made a fine distinction between turtle-doves and wild pigeons; they would have killed wild pigeons if they had got a chance, though you could not tell them from turtle-doves except by their size and the sound they made with their wings. But there were not many pigeons in the woods around the Boy's Town, and they were very shy. There were snipe along the river, and flocks of kildees on the Commons, but the bird that was mostly killed by these boys was the yellowhammer. They distinguished, again, in its case; and decided that it was not a woodpecker, and might be killed; sometimes they thought that woodpeckers were so nearly yellowhammers that they might be killed, but they had never heard of any one's eating a woodpecker, and so they could not quite bring themselves to it. There were said to be squirrels in the hickory woods near the Poor-House, but that was a great way off for my boy; besides the squirrels, there was a cross bull in those woods, and sometimes Solomon Whistler passed through them on his way to or from the Poor-House; so my boy never hunted squirrels. Sometimes he went with his brother for rabbits, which you could track through the corn-fields in a light snow, and sometimes, if they did not turn out to be cats, you could get a shot at them. Now and then there were quail in the wheat-stubble, and there were meadow-larks in the pastures, but they were very wild.

After all, yellowhammers were the chief reliance in the chase; they were pre-occupied, unsuspecting birds, and lit on fence rails and dead trees, so that they were pretty easy to shoot. If you could bring home a yellowhammer you felt that you had something to show for your long day's tramp through the woods and fields, and for the five cents' worth of powder and five cents' worth of shot that you had fired off at other game. Sometimes you just fired it off at mullein-stalks, or barns, or anything you came to. There were a good many things you could do with a gun; you could fire your ramrod out of it, and see it sail through the air; you could fill the muzzle up with water, on top of a charge, and send the water in a straight column at a fence. The boys all believed that you could fire that column of water right through a man, and they always wanted to try whether it would go through a cow, but they were afraid the owner of the cow would find it out. There was a good deal of pleasure in cleaning your gun when it got so foul that your ramrod stuck in it and you could hardly get it out. You poured hot water into the muzzle and blew it through the nipple, till it began to show clear; then you wiped it dry with soft rags wound on your gun-screw, and then oiled it with greasy tow. Sometimes the tow would get loose from the screw, and stay in the barrel, and then you would have to pick enough powder in at the nipple to blow it out. Of course I am talking of the old muzzle-loading shot-gun, which I dare say the boys never use nowadays.

But the great pleasure of all, in hunting, was getting home tired and footsore in the evening, and smelling the supper almost as soon as you came in sight of the house. There was nearly always hot biscuit for supper, with steak, and with coffee such as nobody but a boy's mother ever knew how to make; and just as likely as not there was some kind of preserves; at any rate, there was apple-butter. You could hardly take the time to wash the powder-grime off your hands and face before you rushed to the table; and if you had brought home a yellowhammer you left it with your gun on the back porch, and perhaps the cat got it and saved you the trouble of cleaning it. A cat can clean a bird a good deal quicker than a boy can, and she does not hate to do it half as badly.

Next to the pleasure of getting home from hunting late, was the pleasure of starting early, as my boy and his brother sometimes did, to shoot ducks on the Little Reservoir in the fall. His brother had an alarm-clock, which he set at about four, and he was up the instant it rang, and pulling my boy out of bed, where he would rather have stayed than shot the largest mallard duck in the world. They raked the ashes off the bed of coals in the fireplace, and while the embers ticked and bristled, and flung out little showers of sparks, they hustled on their clothes, and ran down the back stairs into the yard with their guns. Tip, the dog, was already waiting for them there, for he seemed to know they were going that morning, and he began whimpering for joy, and twisting himself sideways up against them, and nearly wagging his tail off; and licking their hands and faces, and kissing their guns all over; he was about crazy. When they started, he knew where they were going, and he rushed ahead through the silent little sleeping town, and led the way across the wide Commons, where the cows lay in dim bulks on the grass, and the geese waddled out of his way with wild clamorous cries, till they came in sight of the Reservoir. Then Tip fell back with my boy and let the elder brother go ahead, for he always had a right to the first shot; and while he dodged down behind the bank, and crept along to the place where the ducks usually were, my boy kept a hold on Tip's collar, and took in the beautiful mystery of the early morning. The place so familiar by day was estranged to his eyes in that pale light, and he was glad of old Tip's company, for it seemed a time when there might very well be ghosts about. The water stretched a sheet of smooth, gray silver, with little tufts of mist on its surface, and through these at last he could see the ducks softly gliding to and fro, and he could catch some dreamy sound from them. His heart stood still and then jumped wildly in his breast, as the still air was startled with the rush of wings, and the water broke with the plunge of other flocks arriving. Then he began to make those bets with himself that a boy hopes he will lose: he bet that his brother would not hit any of them; he bet that he did not even see them; he bet that if he did see them and got a shot at them, they would not come back so that he could get a chance himself to kill any. It seemed to him that he had to wait an hour, and just when he was going to hollo, and tell his brother where the ducks were, the old smoothbore sent out a red flash and a white puff before he heard the report; Tip tore loose from his grasp; and he heard the splashing rise of the ducks, and the hurtling rush of their wings; and he ran forward, yelling, "How many did you hit? Where are they? Where are you? Are they coming back? It's my turn now!" and making an outcry that would have frightened away a fleet of ironclads, but much less a flock of ducks.

One shot always ended the morning's sport, and there were always good reasons why this shot never killed anything.

XIV.
FORAGING.

The foraging began with the first relenting days of winter, which usually came in February. Then the boys began to go to the woods to get sugar-water, as they called the maple sap, and they gave whole Saturdays to it as long as the sap would run. It took at least five or six boys to go for sugar-water, and they always had to get a boy whose father had an auger to come along, so as to have something to bore the trees with. On their way to the woods they had to stop at an elder thicket to get elder-wood to make spiles of, and at a straw pile to cut straws to suck the sap through, if the spiles would not work. They always brought lots of tin buckets to take the sap home in, and the big boys made the little fellows carry these, for they had to keep their own hands free to whittle the elder sticks into the form of spouts, and to push the pith out and make them hollow. They talked loudly and all at once, and they ran a good deal of the way, from the excitement. If it was a good sugar-day, there were patches of snow still in the fence corners and shady places, which they searched for rabbit-tracks; but the air was so warm that they wanted to take their shoes off, and begin going barefoot at once. Overhead, the sky was a sort of pale, milky blue, with the sun burning softly through it, and casting faint shadows. When they got into the woods, it was cooler, and there were more patches of snow, with bird-tracks and squirrel-tracks in them. They could hear the blue-jays snarling at one another, and the yellowhammer chuckling; on some dead tree a redheaded woodpecker hammered noisily, and if the boys had only had a gun with them they could have killed lots of things. Now and then they passed near some woodchoppers, whose axes made a pleasant sound, without frightening any of the wild things, they had got so used to them; sometimes the boys heard the long hollow crash of a tree they were felling. But all the time they kept looking out for a good sugar-tree, and when they saw a maple stained black from the branches down with the sap running from the little holes that the sapsuckers had made, they burst into a shout, and dashed forward, and the fellow with the auger began to bore away, while the other fellows stood round and told him how, and wanted to make him let them do it. Up and down the tree there was a soft murmur from the bees that had found it out before the boys, and every now and then they wove through the air the straight lines of their coming and going, and made the fellows wish they could find a bee-tree. But for the present these were intent upon the sugar-tree, and kept hurrying up the boy with the auger. When he had bored in deep enough, they tried to fit a spile to the hole, but it was nearly always crooked and too big, or else it pointed downward and the water would not run up through the spile. Then some of them got out their straws, and began to suck the sap up from the hole through them, and to quarrel and push, till they agreed to take turn-about, and others got the auger and bunted for another blackened tree. They never could get their spiles to work, and the water gathered so slowly in the holes they bored, and some of the fellows took such long turns, that it was very little fun. They tried to get some good out of the small holes the sap-suckers had made, but there were only a few drops in them, mixed with bark and moss. If it had not been for the woodchoppers, foraging for sugar-water would always have been a failure; but one of them was pretty sure to come up with his axe in his hand, and show the boys how to get the water. He would choose one of the roots near the foot of the tree, and chop a clean, square hole in it; the sap flew at each stroke of his axe, and it rose so fast in the well he made that the thirstiest boy could not keep it down, and three or four boys, with their heads jammed tight together and their straws plunged into its depths, lay stretched upon their stomachs and drank their fill at once. When every one was satisfied, or as nearly satisfied as a boy can ever be, they began to think how they could carry some of the sugar-water home. But by this time it would be pretty late in the afternoon; and they would have to put it off till some other day, when they intended to bring something to dip the water out with; the buckets they had brought were all too big. Then, if they could get enough, they meant to boil it down and make sugar-wax. I never knew of any boys who did so.

The next thing after going for sugar-water was gathering may-apples, as they called the fruit of the mandrake in that country. They grew to their full size, nearly as large as a pullet's egg, some time in June, and they were gathered green, and carried home to be ripened in the cornmeal-barrel. The boys usually forgot about them before they were ripe; when now and then one was remembered, it was a thin, watery, sour thing at the best. But the boys gathered them every spring, in the pleasant open woods where they grew, just beyond the densest shade of the trees, among the tall, straggling grasses; and they had that joyous sense of the bounty of nature in hoarding them up which is one of the sweetest and dearest experiences of childhood. Through this the boy comes close to the heart of the mother of us all, and rejoices in the wealth she never grudges to those who are willing to be merely rich enough.

There were not many wild berries in the country near the Boy's Town, or what seemed near; but sometimes my boy's father took him a great way off to a region, long lost from the map, where there were blackberries. The swimming lasted so late into September, however, that the boys began to go for nuts almost as soon as they left off going into the water. They began with the little acorns that they called chinquepins, and that were such a pretty black, streaked upward from the cup with yellow, that they gathered them half for the unconscious pleasure of their beauty. They were rather bitter, and they puckered your mouth; but still you ate them. They were easy to knock off the low oaks where they grew, and they were so plentiful that you could get a peck of them in no time. There was no need of anybody's climbing a tree to shake them; but one day the boys got to telling what they would do if a bear came, and one of them climbed a chinquepin-tree to show how he would get out on such a small limb that the bear would be afraid to follow him; and he went so far out on the limb that it broke under him. Perhaps he was heavier than he would have been if he had not been carrying the load of guilt which must burden a boy who is playing hookey. At any rate, he fell to the ground, and lay there helpless while the other boys gathered round him, and shared all the alarm he felt for his life. His despair of now hiding the fact that he had been playing hookey was his own affair, but they reasoned with him that the offence would be overlooked in the anxiety which his disaster must arouse. He was prepared to make the most of this, and his groans grew louder as he drew near home in the arms of the boys who took turns, two and two, in carrying him the whole long way from Dayton Lane, with a terrified procession of alternates behind them. These all ran as soon as they came in sight of his house and left the last pair to deliver him to his mother. They never knew whether she forgave him fully, or merely waited till he got well. You never could tell how a boy's mother was going to act in any given case; mothers were so very apt to act differently.

    Red haws came a little before chinquepins. The trees grew mostly by the First Lock, and the boys gathered the haws when they came out from swimming in the canal. They did not take bags to gather haws, as they did chinquepins; the fruit was not thought worthy of that honor; but they filled their pockets with them and ate them on the way home. They were rather nice, with a pleasant taste between a small apple and a rose seed-pod; only you had to throw most of them away because they were wormy. Once when the fellows were gathering haws out there they began to have fun with a flock of turkeys, especially the gobblers, and one boy got an old gobbler to following him while he walked slowly backward, and teased him. The other boys would not have told him for anything when they saw him backing against a low stump. When he reached it, his head went down and his heels flew into the air, and then the gobbler hopped upon him and began to have some of the fun himself. The boys always thought that if they had not rushed up all together and scared the gobbler off, he would have torn the boy to pieces, but very likely he would not. He probably intended just to have fun with him.

    The woods were pretty full of the kind of hickory-trees called pignuts, and the boys gathered the nuts, and even ate their small, bitter kernels; and around the Poor-House woods there were some shag-barks, but the boys did not go for them because of the bull and the crazy people. Their great and constant reliance in foraging was the abundance of black walnuts which grew everywhere, along the roads and on the river-banks, as well as in the woods and the pastures. Long before it was time to go walnutting, the boys began knocking off the nuts and trying whether they were ripe enough; and just as soon as the kernels began to fill out, the fellows began making walnut wagons. I do not know why it was thought necessary to have a wagon to gather walnuts, but I know that it was, and that a boy had to make a new wagon every year. No boy's walnut wagon could last till the next year; it did very well if it lasted till the next day. He had to make it nearly all with his pocket-knife. He could use a saw to block the wheels out of a pine board, and he could use a hatchet to rough off the corners of the blocks, but he had to use his knife to give them any sort of roundness, and they were not very round then; they were apt to be oval in shape, and they always wabbled. He whittled the axles out with his knife, and he made the hubs with it. He could get a tongue ready-made if he used a broom-handle or a hoop-pole, but that had in either case to be whittled so it could be fastened to the wagon; he even bored the linchpin holes with his knife if he could not get a gimlet; and if he could not get an auger, he bored the holes through the wheels with a red-hot poker, and then whittled them large enough with his knife. He had to use pine for nearly everything, because any other wood was too hard to whittle; and then the pine was always splitting. It split in the axles when he was making the linchpin holes, and the wheels had to be kept on by linchpins that were tied in; the wheels themselves split, and had to be strengthened by slats nailed across the rifts. The wagon-bed was a candle-box nailed to the axles, and that kept the front-axle tight, so that it took the whole width of a street to turn a very little wagon in without upsetting.

FORAGING.

When the wagon was all done, the boy who owned it started off with his brothers, or some other boys who had no wagon, to gather walnuts. He started early in the morning of some bright autumn day while the frost still bearded the grass in the back-yard, and bristled on the fence-tops and the roof of the wood-shed, and hurried off to the woods so as to get there before the other boys had got the walnuts. The best place for them was in some woods-pasture where the trees stood free of one another, and around them, in among the tall, frosty grass, the tumbled nuts lay scattered in groups of twos and threes, or fives, some still yellowish-green in their hulls, and some black, but all sending up to the nostrils of the delighted boy the incense of their clean, keen, wild-woody smell, to be a memory forever. The leaves had dropped from the trees overhead, and the branches outlined themselves against the blue sky, and dangled from their outer stems clusters of the unfallen fruit, as large as oranges, and only wanting a touch to send them plumping down into the grass where sometimes their fat hulls burst, and the nuts almost leaped into the boys' hands. The boys ran, some of them to gather the fallen nuts, and others to get clubs and rocks to beat them from the trees; one was sure to throw off his jacket and kick off his shoes and climb the tree to shake every limb where a walnut was still clinging. When they had got them all heaped up like a pile of grape-shot at the foot of the tree, they began to hull them, with blows of a stick, or with stones, and to pick the nuts from the hulls, where the grubs were battening on their assured ripeness, and to toss them into a little heap, a very little heap indeed compared with the bulk of that they came from. The boys gloried in getting as much walnut stain on their hands as they could, for it would not wash off, and it showed for days that they had been walnutting; sometimes they got to staining one another's faces with the juice, and pretending they were Indians.

The sun rose higher and higher, and burned the frost from the grass, and while the boys worked and yelled and chattered they got hotter and hotter, and began to take off their shoes and stockings, till every one of them was barefoot. Then, about three or four o'clock, they would start homeward, with half a bushel of walnuts in their wagon, and their shoes and stockings piled in on top of them. That is, if they had good luck. In a story, they would always have had good luck, and always gone home with half a bushel of walnuts; but this is a history, and so I have to own that they usually went home with about two quarts of walnuts rattling round under their shoes and stockings in the bottom of the wagon. They usually had no such easy time getting them as they always would in a story; they did not find them under the trees, or ready to drop off, but they had to knock them off with about six or seven clubs or rocks to every walnut, and they had to pound the hulls so hard to get the nuts out that sometimes they cracked the nuts. That was because they usually went walnutting before the walnuts were ripe. But they made just as much preparation for drying the nuts on the wood-shed roof whether they got half a gallon or half a bushel; for they did not intend to stop gathering them till they had two or three barrels. They nailed a cleat across the roof to keep them from rolling off, and they spread them out thin, so that they could look more than they were, and dry better. They said they were going to keep them for Christmas, but they had to try pretty nearly every hour or so whether they were getting dry, and in about three days they were all eaten up.

I dare say boys are very different nowadays, and do everything they say they are going to do, and carry out all their undertakings. But in that day they never carried out any of their undertakings. Perhaps they undertook too much; but the failure was a part of the pleasure of undertaking a great deal, and if they had not failed they would have left nothing for the men to do; and a more disgusting thing than a world full of idle men who had done everything there was to do while they were boys, I cannot imagine. The fact is, boys *have* to leave a little for men to do, or else the race would go to ruin; and this almost makes me half believe that perhaps even the boys of the present time may be prevented from doing quite as much as they think they are going to do, until they grow up. Even then they may not want to do it all, but only a small part of it. I have noticed that men do not undertake half so many things as boys do; and instead of wanting to be circus-actors and Indians, and soldiers, and boat-drivers, and politicians and robbers, and to run off, and go in swimming all the time, and out hunting and walnutting, they keep to a very few things, and are glad then if they can do them. It is very curious, but it is true; and I advise any boy who doubts it to watch his father awhile.

XV.
MY BOY.

Every boy is two or three boys, or twenty or thirty different kinds of boys in one; he is all the time living many lives and forming many characters; but it is a good thing if he can keep one life and one character when he gets to be a man. He may turn out to be like an onion when he is grown up, and be nothing but hulls, that you keep peeling off, one after another, till you think you have got down to the heart, at last, and then you have got down to nothing.

All the boys may have been like my boy in the Boy's Town, in having each an inward being that was not the least like their outward being, but that somehow seemed to be their real self, whether it truly was so or not. But I am certain that this was the case with him, and that while he was joyfully sharing the wild sports and conforming to the savage usages of the boy's world about him, he was dwelling in a wholly different world within him, whose wonders no one else knew. I could not tell now these wonders any more than he could have told them then; but it was a world of dreams, of hopes, of purposes, which he would have been more ashamed to avow for himself than I should be to avow for him. It was all vague and vast, and it came out of the books that he read, and that filled his soul with their witchery, and often held him aloof with their charm in the midst of the plays from which they could not lure him wholly away, or at all away. He did not know how or when their enchantment began, and he could hardly recall the names of some of them afterwards. First of them was Goldsmith's "History of Greece," which made him an Athenian of Pericles's time, and Goldsmith's "History of Rome," which naturalized him in a Roman citizenship chiefly employed in slaying tyrants; from the time of Appius Claudius down to the time of Domitian, there was hardly a tyrant that he did not slay. After he had read these books, not once or twice, but twenty times over, his father thought fit to put into his hands "The Travels of Captain Ashe in North America," to encourage, or perhaps to test, his taste for useful reading; but this was a failure. The captain's travels were printed with long esses, and the boy could make nothing of them, for other reasons. The fancy nourished upon

"The glory that was Greece
And the grandeur that was Rome,"

starved amidst the robust plenty of the Englishman's criticisms of our early manners and customs. Neither could money hire the boy to read "Malte-Brun's Geography," in three large folios, of a thousand pages each, for which there was a standing offer of fifty cents from the father, who had never been able to read it himself. But shortly after he failed so miserably with Captain Ashe, the boy came into possession of a priceless treasure. It was that little treatise on "Greek and Roman Mythology" which I have mentioned, and which he must literally have worn out with reading, since no fragment of it seems to have survived his boyhood. Heaven knows who wrote it or published it; his father bought it with a number of other books at an auction, and the boy, who had about that time discovered the chapter on prosody in the back part of his grammar, made poems from it for years, and appeared in many transfigurations, as this and that god and demigod and hero upon imagined occasions in the Boy's Town, to the fancied admiration of all the other fellows. I do not know just why he wished to appear to his grandmother in a vision; now as Mercury with winged feet, now as Apollo with his drawn bow, now as Hercules leaning upon his club and resting from his Twelve Labors. Perhaps it was because he thought that his grandmother, who used to tell the children about her life in Wales, and show them the picture of a castle where she had once slept when she was a girl, would appreciate him in these apotheoses. If he believed they would make a vivid impression upon the sweet old Quaker lady, no doubt he was right.

There was another book which he read about this time, and that was "The Greek Soldier." It was the story of a young Greek, a glorious Athenian, who had fought through the Greek war of independence against the Turks, and then come to America and published the narrative of his adventures. They fired my boy with a retrospective longing to have been present at the Battle of Navarino, when the allied ships of the English, French, and Russians destroyed the Turkish fleet; but it seemed to him that he could not have borne to have the allies impose a king upon the Greeks, when they really wanted a republic, and so he was able to console himself for having been absent. He did what he could in fighting the war over again, and he intended to harden himself for the long struggle by sleeping on the floor, as the Greek soldier had done. But the children often fell asleep on the floor in the warmth of the hearth-fire; and his preparation for the patriotic strife was not distinguishable in its practical effect from a reluctance to go to bed at the right hour.

Captain Riley's narrative of his shipwreck on the coast of Africa, and his captivity among the Arabs, was a book which my boy and his brother prized with a kind of personal interest, because their father told them that he had once seen a son of Captain Riley when he went to get his appointment of collector at Columbus, and that this son was named William Willshire Riley, after the good English merchant, William Willshire, who had ransomed Captain Riley. William Willshire seemed to them almost the best man who ever lived; though my boy had secretly a greater fondness for the Arab, Sidi Hamet, who was kind to Captain Riley and kept his brother Seid from ill-treating him whenever he could. Probably the boy liked him better because the Arab was more picturesque than the Englishman. The whole narrative was very interesting; it had a vein of sincere and earnest piety in it which was not its least charm, and it was written in a style of old-fashioned stateliness which was not without its effect with the boys.

Somehow they did not think of the Arabs in this narrative as of the same race and faith with the Arabs of Bagdad and the other places in the "Arabian Nights." They did not think whether these were Mohammedans or not; they naturalized them in the fairy world where all boys are citizens, and lived with them there upon the same familiar terms as they lived with Robinson Crusoe. Their father once told them that Robinson Crusoe had robbed the real narrative of Alexander Selkirk of the place it ought to have held in the remembrance of the world; and my boy had a feeling of guilt in reading it, as if he were making himself the accomplice of an impostor. He liked the "Arabian Nights," but oddly enough these wonderful tales made no such impression on his fancy as the stories in a wretchedly inferior book made. He did not know the name of this book, or who wrote it; from which I imagine that much of his reading was of the purblind sort that ignorant grown-up people do, without any sort of literary vision. He read this book perpetually, when he was not reading his "Greek and Roman Mythology;" and then suddenly, one day, as happens in childhood with so many things, it vanished out of his possession as if by magic. Perhaps he lost it; perhaps he lent it; at any rate it was gone, and he never got it back, and he never knew what book it was till thirty years afterwards, when he picked up from a friend's library-table a copy of "Gesta Romanorum," and recognized in this collection of old monkish legends the long-missing treasure of his boyhood. These stories, without beauty of invention, without art of construction or character, without spirituality in their crude materialization, which were read aloud in the refectories of mediæval cloisters while the monks sat at meat, laid a spell upon the soul of the boy that governed his life. He conformed his conduct to the principles and maxims which actuated the behavior of the shadowy people of these dry-as-dust tales; he went about drunk with the fumes of fables about Roman emperors that never were, in an empire that never was; and, though they tormented him by putting a mixed and impossible civilization in the place of that he knew from his Goldsmith, he was quite helpless to break from their influence. He was always expecting some wonderful thing to happen to him as things happened there in fulfilment of some saying or prophecy; and at every trivial moment he made sayings and prophecies for himself, which he wished events to fulfil. One Sunday when he was walking in an alley behind one of the stores, he found a fur cap that had probably fallen out of the store-loft window. He ran home with it, and in his simple-hearted rapture he told his mother that as soon as he picked it up there came into his mind the words, "He who picketh up this cap picketh up a fortune," and he could hardly wait for Monday to come and let him restore the cap to its owner and receive an enduring prosperity in reward of his virtue. Heaven knows what form he expected this to take; but when he found himself in the store, he lost all courage; his tongue clove to the roof of his mouth, and he could not utter a syllable of the fine phrases he had made to himself. He laid the cap on the counter without a word; the storekeeper came up and took it in his hand. "What's this?" he said. "Why, this is ours," and he tossed the cap into a loose pile of hats by the showcase, and the boy slunk out, cut to the heart and crushed to the dust. It was such a cruel disappointment and mortification that it was rather a relief to have his brother mock him, and come up and say from time to time, "He who picketh up this cap picketh up a fortune," and then split into a jeering laugh. At least he could fight his brother, and, when he ran, could stone him; and he could throw quads and quoins, and pieces of riglet at the jour printers when the story spread to them, and one of them would begin, "He who picketh—"

He was not different from other boys in his desire to localize, to realize, what he read; and he was always contriving in fancy scenes and encounters of the greatest splendor, in which he bore a chief part. Inwardly he was all thrones, principalities, and powers, the foe of tyrants, the friend of good emperors, and the intimate of magicians, and magnificently apparelled; outwardly he was an incorrigible little sloven, who suffered in all social exigencies from the direst bashfulness, and wished nothing so much as to shrink out of the sight of men if they spoke to him. He could not help revealing sometimes to the kindness of his father and mother the world of foolish dreams one half of him lived in, while the other half swam, and fished, and hunted, and ran races, and played tops and marbles, and squabbled and scuffled in the Boy's Town. Very likely they sympathized with him more than they let him know; they encouraged his reading, and the father directed his taste as far as might be, especially in poetry. The boy liked to make poetry, but he preferred to read prose, though he listened to the poems his father read aloud, so as to learn how they were made. He learned certain pieces by heart, like "The Turk lay dreaming of the hour," and "Pity the sorrows of a poor old man," and he was fond of some passages that his father wished him to know in Thomson's "Seasons." There were some of Moore's songs, too, that he was fond of, such as "When in death I shall calm recline," and "It was noon and on flowers that ranged all around." He learned these by heart, to declaim at school, where he spoke, "On the banks of the Danube fair Adelaide hied," from Campbell; but he could hardly speak the "Soldier's Dream" for the lump that came into his throat at the lines,

"My little ones kissed me a thousand times o'er,
And my wife sobbed aloud in her fulness of heart.

"'Stay, stay with us! Stay! Thou art weary and worn!'
And fain was their war-broken soldier to stay;
But sorrow returned at the dawning of morn,
And the voice in my dreaming ear melted away!"

He was himself both the war-broken soldier and the little ones that kissed him, in the rapture of this now old-fashioned music, and he woke with pangs of heartbreak in the very person of the dreamer.

But he could not make anything either of Byron or Cowper; and he did not even try to read the little tree-calf volumes of Homer and Virgil which his father had in the versions of Pope and Dryden; the small copperplates with which they were illustrated conveyed no suggestion to him. Afterwards he read Goldsmith's "Deserted Village," and he formed a great passion for Pope's "Pastorals," which he imitated in their easy heroics; but till he came to read Longfellow, and Tennyson, and Heine, he never read any long poem without more fatigue than pleasure. His father used to say that the taste for poetry was an acquired taste, like the taste for tomatoes, and that he would come to it yet; but he never came to it, or so much of it as some people seemed to do, and he always had his sorrowful misgivings as to whether they liked it as much as they pretended. I think, too, that it should be a flavor, a spice, a sweet, a delicate relish in the high banquet of literature, and never a chief dish; and I should not know how to defend my boy for trying to make long poems of his own at the very time when he found it so hard to read other people's long poems.

He had no conception of authorship as a vocation in life, and he did not know why he wanted to make poetry. After first flaunting his skill in it before the boys, and getting one of them into trouble by writing a love-letter for him to a girl at school, and making the girl cry at a thing so strange and puzzling as a love-letter in rhyme, he preferred to conceal his gift. It became

"His shame in crowds—his solitary pride,"

and he learned to know that it was considered *soft* to write poetry, as indeed it mostly is. He himself regarded with contempt a young man who had printed a piece of poetry in his father's newspaper and put his own name to it. He did not know what he would not have done sooner than print poetry and put his name to it; and he was melted with confusion when a girl who was going to have a party came to him at the printing-office and asked him to make her the invitations in verse. The printers laughed, and it seemed to the boy that he could never get over it.

But such disgraces are soon lived down, even at ten years, and a great new experience which now came to him possibly helped the boy to forget. This was the theatre, which he had sometimes heard his father speak of. There had once been a theatre in the Boy's Town, when a strolling company came up from Cincinnati, and opened for a season in an empty pork-house. But that was a long time ago, and, though he had written a tragedy, all that the boy knew of a theatre was from a picture in a Sunday-school book where a stage scene was given to show what kind of desperate amusements a person might come to in middle life if he began by breaking the Sabbath in his youth. His brother had once been taken to a theatre in Pittsburgh by one of their river-going uncles, and he often told about it; but my boy formed no conception of the beautiful reality from his accounts of a burglar who jumped from a roof and was chased by a watchman with a pistol up and down a street with houses painted on a curtain.

"THE BEACON OF DEATH."

The company which came to the Boy's Town in his time was again from Cincinnati, and it was under the management of the father and mother of two actresses, afterwards famous, who were then children, just starting upon their career. These pretty little creatures took the leading parts in "Bombastes Furioso," the first night my boy ever saw a play, and he instantly fell impartially in love with both of them, and tacitly remained their abject slave for a great while after. When the smaller of them came out with a large pair of stage boots in one hand and a drawn sword in the other, and said,

"Whoever dares these boots displace
Shall meet Bombastes face to face,"

if the boy had not already been bereft of his senses by the melodrama preceding the burlesque, he must have been transported by her beauty, her grace, her genius. He, indeed, gave her and her sister his heart, but his mind was already gone, rapt from him by the adorable pirate who fought a losing fight with broadswords, two up and two down—click-click, click-click—and died all over the deck of the pirate ship in the opening piece. This was called the "Beacon of Death," and the scene represented the forecastle of the pirate ship with a lantern dangling from the rigging, to lure unsuspecting merchantmen to their doom. Afterwards, the boy remembered nothing of the story, but a scrap of the dialogue meaninglessly remained with him; and when the pirate captain appeared with his bloody crew and said, hoarsely, "Let us go below and get some brandy!" the boy would have bartered all his hopes of bliss to have been that abandoned ruffian. In fact, he always liked, and longed to be, the villain, rather than any other person in the play, and he so glutted himself with crime of every sort in his tender years at the theatre that he afterwards came to be very tired of it, and avoided the plays and novels that had very marked villains in them.

He was in an ecstasy as soon as the curtain rose that night, and he lived somewhere out of his body as long as the playing lasted, which was well on to midnight; for in those days the theatre did not meanly put the public off with one play, but gave it a heartful and its money's worth with three. On his first night my boy saw "The Beacon of Death," "Bombastes Furioso," and "Black-eyed Susan," and he never afterwards saw less than three plays each night, and he never missed a night, as long as the theatre languished in the unfriendly air of that mainly Calvinistic community, where the theatre was regarded by most good people as the eighth of the seven deadly sins. The whole day long he dwelt in a dream of it that blotted out, or rather consumed with more effulgent brightness, all the other day-dreams he had dreamed before, and his heart almost burst with longing to be a villain like those villains on the stage, to have a moustache—a black moustache—such as they wore at a time when every one off the stage was clean shaven, and somehow to end bloodily, murderously, as became a villain.

I dare say this was not quite a wholesome frame of mind for a boy of ten years; but I do not defend it; I only portray it. Being the boy he was, he was destined somehow to dwell half the time in a world of dreamery; and I have tried to express how, when he had once got enough of villainy, he reformed his ideals and rather liked virtue. At any rate, it was a phase of being that could not have been prevented without literally destroying him, and I feel pretty sure that his father did well to let him have his fill of the theatre at once. He could not have known of the riot of emotions behind the child's shy silence, or how continually he was employed in dealing death to all the good people in the pieces he saw or imagined. This the boy could no more have suffered to appear than his passion for those lovely little girls, for whose sake he somehow perpetrated these wicked deeds. The theatre bills, large and small, were printed in his father's office, and sometimes the amiable manager and his wife strolled in with the copy. The boy always wildly hoped and feared they would bring the little girls with them, but they never did, and he contented himself with secretly adoring the father and mother, doubly divine as their parents and as actors. They were on easy terms with the roller-boy, the wretch who shot turtle-doves with no regard for their symbolical character, and they joked with him, in a light give-and-take that smote my boy with an anguish of envy. It would have been richly enough for him to pass the least word with them; a look, a smile from them would have been bliss; but he shrank out of their way; and once when he met them in the street, and they seemed to be going to speak to him, he ran so that they could not.

XVI.
OTHER BOYS.

I cannot quite understand why the theatre, which my boy was so full of, and so fond of, did not inspire him to write plays, to pour them out, tragedy upon tragedy, till the world was filled with tears and blood. Perhaps it was because his soul was so soaked, and, as it were, water-logged with the drama, that it could only drift sluggishly in that welter of emotions, and make for no point, no port, where it could recover itself and direct its powers again. The historical romance which he had begun to write before the impassioned days of the theatre seems to have been lost sight of at this time, though it was an enterprise that he was so confident of carrying forward that he told all his family and friends about it, and even put down the opening passages of it on paper which he cut in large quantity, and ruled himself, so as to have it exactly suitable. The story, as I have said, was imagined from events in Irving's history of the "Conquest of Granada," a book which the boy loved hardly less than the monkish legends of "Gesta Romanorum," and it concerned the rival fortunes of Hamet el Zegri and Boabdil el Chico, the uncle and nephew who vied with each other for the crumbling throne of the Moorish kingdom; but I have not the least notion how it all ended. Perhaps the boy himself had none.

I wish I could truly say that he finished any of his literary undertakings, but I cannot. They were so many that they cumbered the house, and were trodden under foot; and sometimes they brought him to open shame, as when his brother picked one of them up, and began to read it out loud with affected admiration. He was apt to be ashamed of his literary efforts after the first moment, and he shuddered at his brother's burlesque of the high romantic vein in which most of his neverended beginnings were conceived. One of his river-faring uncles was visiting with his family at the boy's home when he laid out the scheme of his great fiction of "Hamet el Zegri," and the kindly young aunt took an interest in it which he poorly rewarded a few months later, when she asked how the story was getting on, and he tried to ignore the whole matter, and showed such mortification at the mention of it that the poor lady was quite bewildered.

The trouble with him was, that he had to live that kind of double life I have spoken of—the Boy's Town life and the Cloud Dweller's life—and that the last, which he was secretly proud of, abashed him before the first. This is always the way with double-lived people, but he did not know it, and he stumbled along through the glory and the ignominy as best he could, and, as he thought, alone.

He was often kept from being a fool, and worse, by that elder brother of his; and I advise every boy to have an elder brother. Have a brother about four years older than yourself, I should say; and if your temper is hot, and your disposition revengeful, and you are a vain and ridiculous dreamer at the same time that you are eager to excel in feats of strength and games of skill, and to do everything that the other fellows do, and are ashamed to be better than the worst boy in the crowd, your brother can be of the greatest use to you, with his larger experience and wisdom. My boy's brother seemed to have an ideal of usefulness, while my boy only had an ideal of glory, to wish to help others, while my boy only wished to help himself. My boy would as soon have thought of his father's doing a wrong thing as of his brother's doing it; and his brother was a calm light of common-sense, of justice, of truth, while he was a fantastic flicker of gaudy purposes which he wished to make shine before men in their fulfilment. His brother was always doing for him and for the younger children; while my boy only did for himself; he had a very gray moustache before he began to have any conception of the fact that he was sent into the world to serve and to suffer, as well as to rule and enjoy. But his brother seemed to know this instinctively; he bore the yoke in his youth, patiently if not willingly; he shared the anxieties as he parted the cares of his father and mother. Yet he was a boy among boys, too; he loved to swim, to skate, to fish, to forage, and passionately, above all, he loved to hunt; but in everything he held himself in check, that he might hold the younger boys in check; and my boy often repaid his conscientious vigilance with hard words and hard names, such as embitter even the most self-forgiving memories. He kept mechanically within certain laws, and though in his rage he hurled every other name at his brother, he would not call him a fool, because then he would be in danger of hell-fire. If he had known just what Raca meant, he might have called him Raca, for he was not so much afraid of the council; but, as it was, his brother escaped that insult, and held through all a rein upon him, and governed him through his scruples as well as his fears.

His brother was full of inventions and enterprises beyond most other boys, and his undertakings came to the same end of nothingness that awaits all boyish endeavor. He intended to make fireworks and sell them; he meant to raise silk-worms; he prepared to take the contract of clearing the new cemetery grounds of stumps by blasting them out with gunpowder. Besides this, he had a plan with another big boy for making money, by getting slabs from the saw-mill, and sawing them up into stove-wood, and selling them to the cooks of canal-boats. The only trouble was that the cooks would not buy the fuel, even when the boys had a half-cord of it all nicely piled up on the canal-bank; they would rather come ashore after dark and take it for nothing. He had a good many other schemes for getting rich, that failed; and he wanted to go to California and dig gold; only his mother would not consent. He really did save the Canal-Basin once, when the banks began to give way after a long rain. He saw the break beginning, and ran to tell his father, who had the firebells rung. The fire companies came rushing to the rescue, but as they could not put the Basin out with their engines, they all got shovels and kept it in. They did not do this before it had overflowed the street, and run into the cellars of the nearest houses. The water stood two feet deep in the kitchen of my boy's house, and the yard was flooded so that the boys made rafts and navigated it for a whole day. My boy's brother got drenched to the skin in the rain, and lots of fellows fell off the rafts.

He belonged to a military company of big boys that had real wooden guns, such as the little boys never could get, and silk oil-cloth caps, and nankeen roundabouts, and white pantaloons with black stripes down the legs; and once they marched out to a boy's that had a father that had a farm, and he gave them all a free dinner in an arbor before the house; bread and butter, and apple-butter, and molasses and pound cake, and peaches and apples; it was splendid. When the excitement about the Mexican War was the highest, the company wanted a fort; and they got a farmer to come and scale off the sod with his plough, in a grassy place there was near a piece of woods, where a good many cows were pastured. They took the pieces of sod, and built them up into the walls of a fort about fifteen feet square; they intended to build them higher than their heads, but they got so eager to have the works stormed that they could not wait, and they commenced having the battle when they had the walls only breast high. There were going to be two parties: one to attack the fort, and the other to defend it, and they were just going to throw sods; but one boy had a real shot-gun, that he was to load up with powder and fire off when the battle got to the worst, so as to have it more like a battle. He thought it would be more like yet if he put in a few shot, and he did it on his own hook. It was a splendid gun, but it would not stand cocked long, and he was resting it on the wall of the fort, ready to fire when the storming-party came on, throwing sods and yelling and holloing; and all at once his gun went off, and a cow that was grazing broadside to the fort gave a frightened bellow, and put up her tail, and started for home. When they found out that the gun, if not the boy, had shot a cow, the Mexicans and Americans both took to their heels; and it was a good thing they did so, for as soon as that cow got home, and the owner found out by the blood on her that she had been shot, though it was only a very slight wound, he was so mad that he did not know what to do, and very likely he would have half killed those boys if he had caught them. He got a plough, and he went out to their fort, and he ploughed it all down flat, so that not one sod remained upon another.

My boy's brother had a good many friends who were too old for my boy to play with. One of them had a father that had a flour-mill out at the First Lock, and for a while my boy's brother intended to be a miller. I do not know why he gave up being one; he did stay up all night with his friend in the mill once, and he found out that the water has more power by night than by day, or at least he came to believe so. He knew another boy who had a father who had a stone-quarry and a canal-boat to bring the stone to town. It was a scow, and it was drawn by one horse; sometimes he got to drive the horse, and once he was allowed to steer the boat. This was a great thing, and it would have been hard to believe of anybody else. The name of the boy that had the father that owned this boat was Piccolo; or, rather, that was his nickname, given him because he could whistle like a piccolo-flute. Once the fellows were disputing whether you could jump halfway across a narrow stream, and then jump back, without touching your feet to the other shore. Piccolo tried it, and sat down in the middle of the stream.

My boy's brother had a scheme for preserving ripe fruit, by sealing it up in a stone jug and burying the jug in the ground, and not digging it up till Christmas. He tried it with a jug of cherries, which he dug up in about a week; but the cherries could not have smelt worse if they had been kept till Christmas. He knew a boy that had a father that had a bakery, and that used to let him come and watch them making bread. There was a fat boy learning the trade there, and they called him the dough-baby, because he looked so white and soft; and the boy whose father had a mill said that down at the German brewery they had a Dutch boy that they were teaching to drink beer, so they could tell how much beer a person could drink if he was taken early; but perhaps this was not true.

My boy's brother went to all sorts of places that my boy was too shy to go to; and he associated with much older boys, but there was one boy who, as I have said, was the dear friend of both of them, and that was the boy who came to learn the trade in their father's printing-office, and who began an historical romance at the time my boy began his great Moorish novel. The first day he came he was put to roll, or ink the types, while my boy's brother worked the press, and all day long my boy, from where he was setting type, could hear him telling the story of a book he had read. It was about a person named Monte Cristo, who was a count, and who could do anything. My boy listened with a gnawing literary jealousy of a boy who had read a book that he had never heard of. He tried to think whether it sounded as if it were as great a book as the "Conquest of Granada," or "Gesta Romanorum;" and for a time he kept aloof from this boy because of his envy. Afterwards they came together on "Don Quixote," but though my boy came to have quite a passionate fondness for him, he was long in getting rid of his grudge against him for his knowledge of "Monte Cristo." He was as great a laughter as my boy and his brother, and he liked the same sports, so that two by two, or all three together, they had no end of jokes and fun. He became the editor of a country newspaper, with varying fortunes but steadfast principles, and when the war broke out he went as a private soldier. He soon rose to be an officer, and fought bravely in many battles. Then he came back to a country-newspaper office where, ever after, he continued to fight the battles of right against wrong, till he died not long ago at his post of duty—a true, generous, and lofty soul. He was one of those boys who grow into the men who seem commoner in America than elsewhere, and who succeed far beyond our millionaires and statesmen in realizing the ideal of America in their nobly simple lives. If his story could be faithfully written out, word for word, deed for deed, it would be far more thrilling than that of Monte Cristo, or any hero of romance; and so would the common story of any common life; but we cannot tell these stories, somehow.

My boy knew nearly a hundred boys, more or less; but it is no use trying to tell about them, for all boys are a good deal alike, and most of these did not differ much from the rest. They were pretty good fellows; that is to say, they never did half the mischief they intended to do, and they had moments of intending to do right, or at least they thought they did, and when they did wrong they said they did not intend to. But my boy never had any particular friend among his schoolmates, though he played and fought with them on intimate terms, and was a good comrade with any boy that wanted to go in swimming or out hunting. His closest friend was a boy who was probably never willingly at school in his life, and who had no more relish of literature or learning in him than the open fields, or the warm air of an early spring day. I dare say it was a sense of his kinship with nature that took my boy with him, and rested his soul from all its wild dreams and vain imaginings. He was like a piece of the genial earth, with no more hint of toiling or spinning in him; willing for anything, but passive, and without force or aim. He lived in a belated log-cabin that stood in the edge of a corn-field on the river-bank, and he seemed, one day when my boy went to find him there, to have a mother, who smoked a cob-pipe, and two or three large sisters who hulked about in the one dim, low room. But the boys had very little to do with each other's houses, or, for that matter, with each other's yards. His friend seldom entered my boy's gate, and never his door; for with all the toleration his father felt for every manner of human creature, he could not see what good the boy was to get from this queer companion. It is certain that, he got no harm; for his companion was too vague and void even to think evil. Socially, he was as low as the ground under foot, but morally he was as good as any boy in the Boy's Town, and he had no bad impulses. He had no impulses at all, in fact, and of his own motion he never did anything, or seemed to think anything. When he wished to get at my boy, he simply appeared in the neighborhood, and hung about the outside of the fence till he came out. He did not whistle, or call "E-oo-we!" as the other fellows did, but waited patiently to be discovered, and to be gone off with wherever my boy listed. He never had any plans himself, and never any will but to go in swimming; he neither hunted nor foraged; he did not even fish; and I suppose that money could not have hired him to run races. He played marbles, but not very well, and he did not care much for the game. The two boys soaked themselves in the river together, and then they lay on the sandy shore, or under some tree, and talked; but my boy could not have talked to him about any of the things that were in his books, or the fume of dreams they sent up in his mind. He must rather have soothed against his soft, caressing ignorance the ache of his fantastic spirit, and reposed his intensity of purpose in that lax and easy aimlessness. Their friendship was not only more innocent than any other friendship my boy had, but it was wholly innocent; they loved each other, and that was all; and why people love one another there is never any satisfactory telling. But this friend of his must have had great natural good in him; and if I could find a man of the make of that boy I am sure I should love him.

My boy's other friends wondered at his fondness for him, and it was often made a question with him at home, if not a reproach to him; so that in the course of time it ceased to be that comfort it had been to him. He could not give him up, but he could not help seeing that he was ignorant and idle, and in a fatal hour he resolved to reform him. I am not able now to say just how he worked his friend up to the point of coming to school, and of washing his hands and feet and face, and putting on a new check shirt to come in. But one day he came, and my boy, as he had planned, took him into his seat, and owned his friendship with him before the whole school. This was not easy, for though everybody knew how much the two were together, it was a different thing to sit with him as if he thought him just as good as any boy, and to help him get his lessons, and stay him mentally as well as socially. He struggled through one day, and maybe another; but it was a failure from the first moment, and my boy breathed freer when his friend came one half-day, and then never came again. The attempted reform had spoiled their simple and harmless intimacy. They never met again upon the old ground of perfect trust and affection. Perhaps the kindly earth-spirit had instinctively felt a wound from the shame my boy had tried to brave out, and shrank from their former friendship without quite knowing why. Perhaps it was my boy who learned to realize that there could be little in common but their common humanity between them, and could not go back to that. At any rate, their friendship declined from this point; and it seems to me, somehow, a pity.

Among the boys who were between my boy and his brother in age was one whom all the boys liked, because he was clever with everybody, with little boys as well as big boys. He was a laughing, pleasant fellow, always ready for fun, but he never did mean things, and he had an open face that made a friend of every one who saw him. He had a father that had a house with a lightning-rod, so that if you were in it when there was a thunder-storm you could not get struck by lightning, as my boy once proved by being in it when there was a thunder-storm and not getting struck. This in itself was a great merit, and there were grape-arbors and peach-trees in his yard which added to his popularity, with cling-stone peaches almost as big as oranges on them. He was a fellow who could take you home to meals whenever he wanted to, and he liked to have boys stay all night with him; his mother was as clever as he was, and even the sight of his father did not make the fellows want to go and hide. His father was so clever that he went home with my boy one night about midnight when the boy had come to pass the night with his boys, and the youngest of them had said he always had the nightmare and walked in his sleep, and as likely as not he might kill you before he knew it. My boy tried to sleep, but the more he reflected upon his chances of getting through the night alive the smaller they seemed; and so he woke up his potential murderer from the sweetest and soundest slumber, and said he was going home, but he was afraid; and the boy had to go and wake his father. Very few fathers would have dressed up and gone home with a boy at midnight, and perhaps this one did so only because the mother made him; but it shows how clever the whole family was.

It was their oldest boy whom my boy and his brother chiefly went with before that boy who knew about "Monte Cristo" came to learn the trade in their father's office. One Saturday in July they three spent the whole day together. It was just the time when the apples are as big as walnuts on the trees, and a boy wants to try whether any of them are going to be sweet or not. The boys tried a great many of them, in an old orchard thrown open for building-lots behind my boy's yard; but they could not find any that were not sour; or that they could eat till they thought of putting salt on them; if you put salt on it, you could eat any kind of green apple, whether it was going to be a sweet kind or not. They went up to the Basin bank and got lots of salt out of the holes in the barrels lying there, and then they ate all the apples they could hold, and after that they cut limber sticks off the trees, and sharpened the points, and stuck apples on them and threw them. You could send an apple almost out of sight that way, and you could scare a dog almost as far as you could see him.

On Monday my boy and his brother went to school, but the other boy was not there, and in the afternoon they heard he was sick. Then, towards the end of the week they heard that he had the flux; and on Friday, just before school let out, the teacher—it was the one that whipped so, and that the fellows all liked—rapped on his desk, and began to speak very solemnly to the scholars. He told them that their little mate, whom they had played with and studied with, was lying very sick, so very sick that it was expected he would die; and then he read them a serious lesson about life and death, and tried to make them feel how passing and uncertain all things were, and resolve to live so that they need never be afraid to die.

Some of the fellows cried, and the next day some of them went to see the dying boy, and my boy went with them. His spirit was stricken to the earth, when he saw his gay, kind playmate lying there, white as the pillow under his wasted face, in which his sunken blue eyes showed large and strange. The sick boy did not say anything that the other boys could hear, but they could see the wan smile that came to his dry lips, and the light come sadly into his eyes, when his mother asked him if he knew this one or that; and they could not bear it, and went out of the room.

In a few days they heard that he was dead, and one afternoon school did not keep, so that the boys might go to the funeral. Most of them walked in the procession; but some of them were waiting beside the open grave, that was dug near the grave of that man who believed there was a hole through the earth from pole to pole, and had a perforated stone globe on top of his monument.

XVII.

FANTASIES AND SUPERSTITIONS.

My boy used to be afraid of this monument, which stood a long time, or what seemed to him a long time, in the yard of the tombstone cutter before it was put up at the grave of the philosopher who imagined the earth as hollow as much of the life is on it. He was a brave officer in the army which held the region against the Indians in the pioneer times; he passed the latter part of his life there, and he died and was buried in the Boy's Town. My boy had to go by the yard when he went to see his grandmother, and even at high noon the sight of the officer's monument, and the other gravestones standing and leaning about, made his flesh creep and his blood run cold. When there were other boys with him he would stop at the door of the shed, where a large, fair German was sawing slabs of marble with a long saw that had no teeth, and that he eased every now and then with water from a sponge he kept by him; but if the boy was alone, and it was getting at all late in the afternoon, he always ran by the place as fast as he could. He could hardly have told what he was afraid of, but he must have connected the gravestones with ghosts.

"HE ALWAYS RAN BY THE PLACE AS FAST AS HE COULD."

His superstitions were not all of the ghastly kind; some of them related to conduct and character. It was noted long ago how boys throw stones, for instance, at a tree, and feign to themselves that this thing or that, of great import, will happen or not as they hit or miss the tree. But my boy had other fancies, which came of things he had read and half understood. In one of his school-books was a story that began, "Charles was an honest boy, but Robert was the name of a thief," and it went on to show how Charles grew up in the respect and affection of all who knew him by forbearing to steal some oranges which their owner had set for safe-keeping at the heels of his horse, while Robert was kicked at once (there was a picture that showed him holding his stomach with both hands), and afterwards came to a bad end, through attempting to take one. My boy conceived from the tale that the name of Robert was necessarily associated with crime; it was long before he outgrew the prejudice; and this tale and others of a like vindictive virtuousness imbued him with such a desire to lead an upright life that he was rather a bother to his friends with his scruples. A girl at school mislaid a pencil which she thought she had lent him, and he began to have a morbid belief that he must have stolen it; he became frantic with the mere dread of guilt; he could not eat or sleep, and it was not till he went to make good the loss with a pencil which his grandfather gave him that the girl said she had found her pencil in her desk, and saved him from the despair of a self-convicted criminal. After that his father tried to teach him the need of using his reason as well as his conscience concerning himself, and not to be a little simpleton. But he was always in an anguish to restore things to their owners, like the good boys in the story-books, and he suffered pangs of the keenest remorse for the part he once took in the disposition of a piece of treasure-trove. This was a brown-paper parcel which he found behind a leaning gravestone in the stone-cutter's yard, and which he could not help peeping into. It was full of raisins, and in the amaze of such a discovery he could not help telling the other boys. They flocked round and swooped down upon the parcel like birds of prey, and left not a raisin behind. In vain he implored them not to stain their souls with this misdeed; neither the law nor the prophets availed; neither the awful shadow of the prison which he cast upon them, nor the fear of the last judgment which he invoked. They said that the raisins did not belong to anybody; that the owner had forgotten all about them; that they had just been put there by some one who never intended to come back for them. He went away sorrowing, without touching a raisin (he felt that the touch must have stricken him with death), and far heavier in soul than the hardened accomplices of his sin, of whom he believed himself the worst in having betrayed the presence of the raisins to them.

He used to talk to himself when he was little, but one day his mother said to him jokingly, "Don't you know that he who talks to himself has the devil for a listener?" and after that he never dared whisper above his breath when he was alone, though his father and mother had both taught him that there was no devil but his own evil will. He shuddered when he heard a dog howling in the night, for that was a sign that somebody was going to die. If he heard a hen crow, as a hen sometimes unnaturally would, he stoned her, because it was a sign of the worst kind of luck. He believed that warts came from playing with toads, but you could send them away by saying certain words over them; and he was sorry that he never had any warts, so that he could send them away, and see them go; but he never could bear to touch a toad, and so of course he could not have warts. Other boys played with toads just to show that they were not afraid of having warts; but every one knew that if you killed a toad, your cow would give bloody milk. I dare say the far forefathers of the race knew this too, when they first began to herd their kine in the birthplace of the Aryan peoples; and perhaps they learned then that if you killed a snake early in the day its tail would live till sundown. My boy killed every snake he could; he thought it somehow a duty; all the boys thought so; they dimly felt that they were making a just return to the serpent-tribe for the bad behavior of their ancestor in the Garden of Eden. Once, in a corn-field near the Little Reservoir, the boys found on a thawing day of early spring knots and bundles of snakes writhen and twisted together, in the torpor of their long winter sleep. It was a horrible sight, that afterwards haunted my boy's dreams. He had nightmares which remained as vivid in his thoughts as anything that happened to him by day. There were no poisonous snakes in the region of the Boy's Town, but there were some large blacksnakes, and the boys said that if a blacksnake got the chance he would run up your leg, and tie himself round your body so that you could not breathe. Nobody had ever seen a blacksnake do it, and nobody had ever seen a hoop-snake, but the boys believed there was such a snake, and that he would take his tail in his mouth, when he got after a person, and roll himself along swifter than the fastest race-horse could run. He did not bite, but when he came up with you he would take the point of his tail out of his mouth and strike it into you. If he struck his tail into a tree, the tree would die. My boy had seen a boy who had been chased by a hoop-snake, but he had not seen the snake, though for the matter of that the boy who had been chased by it had not seen it either; he did not stop to see it. Another kind of snake that was very strange was a hair-snake. No one had ever seen it happen, but every one knew that if you put long horsehairs into a puddle of water and let them stay, they would turn into hair-snakes; and when you drank out of a spring you had to be careful not to swallow a hair-snake, or it would remain in your stomach and grow there.

When you saw a lizard, you had to keep your mouth tight shut, or else the lizard would run down your throat before you knew it. That was what all the boys said, and my boy believed it, though he had never heard of anybody that it happened to. He believed that if you gave a chicken-cock burnt brandy it could lay eggs, and that if you gave a boy burnt brandy it would stop his growing. That was the way the circus-men got their dwarfs, and the India-rubber man kept himself limber by rubbing his joints with rattlesnake oil.

A snake could charm a person, and when you saw a snake you had to kill it before it could get its eye on you or it would charm you. Snakes always charmed birds; and there were mysterious powers of the air and forces of nature that a boy had to be on his guard against, just as a bird had to look out for snakes. You must not kill a granddaddy-long-legs, or a lady-bug; it was bad luck. My boy believed, or was afraid he believed, that

"What you dream Monday morning before daylight
Will come true before Saturday night,"

but if it was something bad, you could keep it from coming true by not telling your dream till you had eaten breakfast. He governed his little, foolish, frightened life not only by the maxims he had learned out of his "Gesta Romanorum," but by common sayings of all sorts, such as

"See a pin and leave it lay
You'll have bad luck all the day,"

and if ever he tried to rebel against this slavery, and went by a pin in the path, his fears tormented him till he came back and picked it up. He would not put on his left stocking first, for that was bad luck; but besides these superstitions, which were common to all the boys, he invented superstitions of his own, with which he made his life a burden. He did not know why, but he would not step upon the cracks between the paving-stones, and some days he had to touch every tree or post along the sidewalk, as Doctor Johnson did in his time, though the boy had never heard of Doctor Johnson then.

While he was yet a very little fellow, he had the distorted, mistaken piety of childhood. He had an abject terror of dying, but it seemed to him that if a person could die right in the centre isle of the church—the Methodist church where his mother used to go before she became finally a New Churchwoman—the chances of that person's going straight to heaven would be so uncommonly good that he need have very little anxiety about it. He asked his mother if she did not think so too, holding by her hand as they came out of church together, and he noticed the sort of gravity and even pain with which she and his father received this revelation of his darkling mind. They tried to teach him what they thought of such things; but though their doctrine caught his fancy and flattered his love of singularity, he was not proof against the crude superstitions of his mates. He thought for a time that there was a Bad Man, but this belief gave way when he heard his father laughing about a certain clergyman who believed in a personal devil.

The boys said the world was going to be burned up some time, and my boy expected the end with his full share of the trouble that it must bring to every sinner. His fears were heightened by the fact that his grandfather believed this end was very near at hand, and was prepared for the second coming of Christ at any moment. Those were the days when the minds of many were stirred by this fear or hope; the believers had their ascension robes ready, and some gave away their earthly goods so as not to be cumbered with anything in their heavenward flight. At home, my boy heard his father jest at the crazy notion, and make fun of the believers; but abroad, among the boys, he took the tint of the prevailing gloom. One awful morning at school, it suddenly became so dark that the scholars could not see to study their lessons, and then the boys knew that the end of the world was coming. There were no clouds, as for a coming storm, but the air was blackened almost to the dusk of night; the school was dismissed, and my boy went home to find the candles lighted, and a strange gloom and silence on everything outside. He remembered entering into this awful time, but he no more remembered coming out of it than if the earth had really passed away in fire and smoke.

He early heard of forebodings and presentiments, and he tried hard against his will to have them, because he was so afraid of having them. For the same reason he did his best, or his worst, to fall into a trance, in which he should know everything that was going on about him, all the preparations for his funeral, all the sorrow and lamentation, but should be unable to move or speak, and only be saved at the last moment by some one putting a mirror to his lips and finding a little blur of mist on it. Sometimes when he was beginning to try to write things and to imagine characters, if he imagined a character's dying, then he became afraid he was that character, and was going to die.

Once, he woke up in the night and found the full moon shining into his room in a very strange and phantasmal way, and washing the floor with its pale light, and somehow it came into his mind that he was going to die when he was sixteen years old. He could then only have been nine or ten, but the perverse fear sank deep into his soul, and became an increasing torture till he passed his sixteenth birthday and entered upon the year in which he had appointed himself to die. The agony was then too great for him to bear alone any longer, and with shame he confessed his doom to his father. "Why," his father said, "you are in your seventeenth year now. It is too late for you to die at sixteen," and all the long-gathering load of misery dropped from the boy's soul, and he lived till his seventeenth birthday and beyond it without further trouble. If he had known that he would be in his seventeenth year as soon as he was sixteen, he might have arranged his presentiment differently.

XVIII.
THE NATURE OF BOYS.

I tell these things about my boy, not so much because they were peculiar to him as because I think they are, many of them, common to all boys. One tiresome fact about boys is that they are so much alike; or used to be. They did not wish to be so, but they could not help it. They did not even know they were alike; and my boy used to suffer in ways that he believed no boy had ever suffered before; but as he grew older he found that boys had been suffering in exactly the same way from the beginning of time. In the world you will find a great many grown-up boys, with gray beards and grandchildren, who think that they have been different their whole lives through from other people, and are the victims of destiny. That is because with all their growing they have never grown to be men, but have remained a sort of cry-babies. The first thing you have to learn here below is that in essentials you are just like every one else, and that you are different from others only in what is not so much worth while. If you have anything in common with your fellow-creatures, it is something that God gave you; if you have anything that seems quite your own, it is from your silly self, and is a sort of perversion of what came to you from the Creator who made you out of himself, and had nothing else to make any one out of. There is not really any difference between you and your fellow-creatures; but only a seeming difference that flatters and cheats you with a sense of your strangeness, and makes you think you are a remarkable fellow.

There is a difference between boys and men, but it is a difference of self-knowledge chiefly. A boy wants to do everything because he does not know he cannot; a man wants to do something because he knows he cannot do everything; a boy always fails, and a man sometimes succeeds because the man knows and the boy does not know. A man is better than a boy because he knows better; he has learned by experience that what is a harm to others is a greater harm to himself, and he would rather not do it. But a boy hardly knows what harm is, and he does it mostly without realizing that it hurts. He cannot invent anything, he can only imitate; and it is easier to imitate evil than good. You can imitate war, but how are you going to imitate peace? So a boy passes his leisure in contriving mischief. If you get another fellow to walk into a wasp's camp, you can see him jump and hear him howl, but if you do not, then nothing at all happens. If you set a dog to chase a cat up a tree, then something has been done; but if you do not set the dog on the cat, then the cat just lies in the sun and sleeps, and you lose your time. If a boy could find out some way of doing good, so that he could be active in it, very likely he would want to do good now and then; but as he cannot, he very seldom wants to do good.

Or at least he did not want to do good in my boy's time. Things may be changed now, for I have been talking of boys as they were in the Boy's Town forty years ago. For anything that I really know to the contrary, a lot of fellows when they get together now may plot good deeds of all kinds, but when more than a single one of them was together then they plotted mischief. When I see five or six boys now lying under a tree on the grass, and they fall silent as I pass them, I have no right to say that they are not arranging to go and carry some poor widow's winter wood into her shed and pile it neatly up for her, and wish to keep it a secret from everybody; but forty years ago I should have had good reason for thinking that they were debating how to tie a piece of her clothes-line along the ground so that when her orphan boy came out for an armload of wood after dark, he would trip on it and send his wood flying all over the yard.

This would not be a sign that they were morally any worse than the boys who read *Harper's Young People*, and who would every one die rather than do such a cruel thing, but that they had not really thought much about it. I dare say that if a crowd of the *Young People*'s readers, from eight to eleven years old, got together, they would choose the best boy among them to lead them on in works of kindness and usefulness; but I am very sorry to say that in the Boy's Town such a crowd of boys would have followed the lead of the worst boy as far as they dared. Not all of them would have been bad, and the worst of them would not have been very bad; but they would have been restless and thoughtless. I am not ready to say that boys now are not wise enough to be good; but in that time and town they certainly were not. In their ideals and ambitions they were foolish, and in most of their intentions they were mischievous. Without realizing that it was evil, they meant more evil than it would have been possible for ten times as many boys to commit. If the half of it were now committed by men, the United States would be such an awful place that the decent people would all want to go and live in Canada.

I have often read in stories of boys who were fond of nature, and loved her sublimity and beauty, but I do not believe boys are ever naturally fond of nature. They want to make use of the woods and fields and rivers; and when they become men they find these aspects of nature endeared to them by association, and so they think that they were dear for their own sakes; but the taste for nature is as purely acquired as the taste for poetry or the taste for tomatoes. I have often seen boys wondering at the rainbow, but it was wonder, not admiration that moved them; and I have seen them excited by a storm, but because the storm was tremendous, not because it was beautiful.

I never knew a boy who loved flowers, or cared for their decorative qualities; if any boy had gathered flowers the other boys would have laughed at him; though boys gather every kind of thing that they think will be of the slightest use or profit. I do not believe they appreciate the perfume of flowers, and I am sure that they never mind the most noisome stench or the most loathsome sight. A dead horse will draw a crowd of small boys, who will dwell without shrinking upon the details of his putrefaction, when they would pass by a rose-tree in bloom with indifference. Hideous reptiles and insects interest them more than the loveliest form of leaf or blossom. Their senses have none of the delicacy which they acquire in after-life.

They are not cruel, that is, they have no delight in giving pain, as a general thing; but they do cruel things out of curiosity, to see how their victims will act. Still, even in this way, I never saw many cruel things done. If another boy gets hurt they laugh, because it is funny to see him hop or hear him yell; but they do not laugh because they enjoy his pain, though they do not pity him unless they think he is badly hurt; then they are scared, and try to comfort him. To bait a hook they tear an angle-worm into small pieces, or impale a grub without flinching; they go to the slaughter-house and see beeves knocked in the head without a tremor. They acquaint themselves, at any risk, with all that is going on in the great strange world they have come into; and they do not pick or choose daintily among the facts and objects they encounter. To them there is neither foul nor fair, clean nor unclean. They have not the least discomfort from being dirty or unkempt, and they certainly find no pleasure in being washed and combed and clad in fresh linen. They do not like to see other boys so; if a boy looking sleek and smooth came among the boys that my boy went with in the Boy's Town, they made it a reproach to him, and hastened to help him spoil his clothes and his nice looks. Some of those boys had hands as hard as horn, cracked open at the knuckles and in the palms, and the crevices blackened with earth or grime; and they taught my boy to believe that he was an inferior and unmanly person, almost of the nature of a cry-baby, because his hands were not horn-like, and cracked open, and filled with dirt.

He had comrades enough and went with everybody, but till he formed that friendship with the queer fellow whom I have told of, he had no friend among the boys; and I very much doubt whether small boys understand friendship, or can feel it as they do afterwards, in its tenderness and unselfishness. In fact they have no conception of generosity. They are wasteful with what they do not want at the moment; but their instinct is to get and not to give. In the Boy's Town, if a fellow appeared at his gate with a piece of bread spread with apple-butter and sugar on top, the other fellows flocked round him and tried to flatter him out of bites of it, though they might be at that moment almost bursting with surfeit. To get a bite was so much clear gain, and when they had wheedled one from the owner of the bread, they took as large a bite as their mouths could stretch to, and they had neither shame nor regret for their behavior, but mocked his just resentment.

The instinct of getting, of hoarding, was the motive of all their foraging; they had no other idea of property than the bounty of nature; and this was well enough as far as it went, but their impulse was not to share this bounty with others, but to keep it each for himself. They hoarded nuts and acorns, and hips and haws, and then they wasted them; and they hoarded other things merely from the greed of getting, and with no possible expectation of advantage. It might be well enough to catch bees in hollyhocks, and imprison them in underground cells with flowers for them to make honey from; but why accumulate fire-flies and even dor-bugs in small brick pens? Why heap together mussel-shells; and what did a boy expect to do with all the marbles he won? You could trade marbles for tops, but they were not money, like pins; and why were pins money? Why did the boys instinctively choose them for their currency, and pay everything with them? There were certain very rigid laws about them, and a bent pin could not be passed among the boys any more than a counterfeit coin among men. There were fixed prices; three pins would buy a bite of apple; six pins would pay your way into a circus; and so on. But where did these pins come from or go to; and what did the boys expect to do with them all? No boy knew. From time to time several boys got together and decided to keep store, and then other boys decided to buy of them with pins; but there was no calculation in the scheme; and though I have read of boys, especially in English books, who made a profit out of their fellows, I never knew any boy who had enough forecast to do it. They were too wildly improvident for anything of the kind, and if they had any virtue at all it was scorn of the vice of stinginess.

They were savages in this as in many other things, but noble savages; and they were savages in such bravery as they showed. That is, they were venturesome, but not courageous with the steadfast courage of civilized men. They fought, and then ran; and they never fought except with some real or fancied advantage. They were grave, like Indians, for the most part; and they were noisy without being gay. They seldom laughed, except at the pain or shame of some one; I think they had no other conception of a joke, though they told what they thought were funny stories, mostly about some Irishman just come across the sea, but without expecting any one to laugh. In fact, life was a very serious affair with them. They lived in a state of outlawry, in the midst of invisible terrors, and they knew no rule but that of might.

I am afraid that *Harper's Young People*, or rather the mothers of *Harper's Young People*, may think I am painting a very gloomy picture of the natives of the Boy's Town; but I do not pretend that what I say of the boys of forty years ago is true of boys nowadays, especially the boys who read *Harper's Young People*. I understand that these boys always like to go tidily dressed and to keep themselves neat; and that a good many of them carry canes. They would rather go to school than fish, or hunt, or swim, any day; and if one of their teachers were ever to offer them a holiday, they would reject it by a vote of the whole school. They never laugh at a fellow when he hurts himself or tears his clothes. They are noble and self-sacrificing friends, and they carry out all their undertakings. They often have very exciting adventures such as my boy and his mates never had; they rescue one another from shipwreck and Indians; and if ever they are caught in a burning building, or cast away on a desolate island, they know just exactly what to do.

But, I am ashamed to say, it was all very different in the Boy's Town; and I might as well make a clean breast of it while I am about it. The fellows in that town were every one dreadfully lazy—that is, they never wanted to do any thing they were set to do; but if they set themselves to do anything, they would work themselves to death at it. In this alone I understand that they differed by a whole world's difference from the boys who read *Harper's Young People*. I am almost afraid to confess how little moral strength most of those long-ago boys had. A fellow would be very good at home, really and truly good, and as soon as he got out with the other fellows he would yield to almost any temptation to mischief that offered, and if none offered he would go and hunt one up, and would never stop till he had found one, and kept at it till it overcame him. The spirit of the boy's world is not wicked, but merely savage, as I have often said in this book; it is the spirit of not knowing better. That is, the prevailing spirit is so. Here and there a boy does know better, but he is seldom a leader among boys; and usually he is ashamed of knowing better, and rarely tries to do better than the rest. He would like to please his father and mother, but he dreads the other boys and what they will say; and so the light of home

fades from his ignorant soul, and leaves him in the outer darkness of the s
that it must be so; but it seems a great pity; and it seems somehow as if th
mother might keep with him in some word, some thought, and be there to
against himself, whenever he is weak and wavering. The trouble is that th
mother are too often children in their way, and little more fit to be the guide than he.

But while I am owning to a good deal that seems to me lamentably wrong in the behavior of the Boy's Town boys, I ought to remember one or two things to their credit. They had an ideal of honor, false enough as far as resenting insult went, but true in some other things. They were always respectful to women, and if a boy's mother ever appeared among them, to interfere in behalf of her boy when they were abusing him, they felt the indecorum, but they were careful not to let her feel it. They would not have dreamed of uttering a rude or impudent word to her; they obeyed her, and they were even eager to serve her, if she asked a favor of them.

For the most part, also, they were truthful, and they only told lies when they felt obliged to do so, as when they had been in swimming and said they had not, or as when they wanted to get away from some of the boys, or did not wish the whole crowd to know what they were doing. But they were generally shamefaced in these lies; and the fellows who could lie boldly and stick to it were few. In the abstract lying was held in such contempt that if any boy said you were a liar you must strike him. That was not to be borne for an instant, any more than if he had called you a thief.

I never knew a boy who was even reputed to have stolen anything, among all the boys, high and low, who met together and played in a perfect social equality; and cheating in any game was despised. To break bounds, to invade an orchard or garden, was an adventure which might be permitted; but even this was uncommon, and most of the boys saw the affair in the true light, and would not take part in it, though it was considered fair to knock apples off a tree that hung over the fence; and if you were out walnutting you might get over the fence in extreme cases, and help yourself. If the owner of the orchard was supposed to be stingy you might do it to plague him. But the standard of honesty was chivalrously high among those boys; and I believe that if ever we have the equality in this world which so many good men have hoped for, theft will be unknown. Dishonesty was rare even among men in the Boy's Town, because there was neither wealth nor poverty there, and all had enough and few too much.

XIX.
THE TOWN ITSELF.

Of course I do not mean to tell what the town was as men knew it, but only as it appeared to the boys who made use of its opportunities for having fun. The civic centre was the court-house, with the county buildings about it in the court-house yard; and the great thing in the court-house was the town clock. It was more important in the boys' esteem than even the wooden woman, who had a sword in one hand and a pair of scales in the other. Her eyes were blinded; and the boys believed that she would be as high as a house if she stood on the ground. She was above the clock, which was so far up in the air, against the summer sky which was always blue, that it made your neck ache to look up at it; and the bell was so large that once when my boy was a very little fellow, and was in the belfry with his brother, to see if they could get some of the pigeons that nested there, and the clock began to strike, it almost smote him dead with the terror of its sound, and he felt his heart quiver with the vibration of the air between the strokes. It seemed to him that he should never live to get down; and he never knew how he did get down. He could remember being in the court-house after that, one night when a wandering professor gave an exhibition in the court-room, and showed the effects of laughing-gas on such men and boys as were willing to breathe it. It was the same gas that dentists now give when they aw teeth; but it was then used to make people merry and truthful, to make them laugh and say just what they thought. My boy was too young to know whether it did either; but he was exactly the right age, when on another night there was a large picture of Death on a Pale Horse shown, to be harrowed to the bottom of his soul by its ghastliness. When he was much older, his father urged him to go to the court-house and hear the great Corwin, whose Mexican War speech he had learned so much of by heart, arguing a case; but the boy was too bashful to go in when he got to the door, and came back and reported that he was afraid they would make him swear. He was sometimes in the court-house yard, at elections and celebrations; and once he came from school at recess with some other boys and explored the region of the jail. Two or three prisoners were at the window, and they talked to the boys and joked; and the boys ran off again and played; and the prisoners remained like unreal things in my boy's fancy. Perhaps if it were not for this unreality which misery puts on for the happy when it is out of sight, no one could be happy in a world where there is so much misery.

The school was that first one which he went to, in the basement of a church. It was the Episcopal church, and he struggled for some meaning in the word Episcopal; he knew that the Seceder church was called so because the spire was cedar; a boy who went to Sunday-school there told him so. There was a Methodist church, where his grandfather went; and a Catholic church, where that awful figure on the cross was. No doubt there were other churches; but he had nothing to do with them.

Besides his grandfather's drug and book store, there was another drug store, and there were eight or ten dry-goods stores, where every spring the boys were taken to be fitted with new straw hats; but the store that they knew best was a toy-store near the market-house, kept by a quaint old German, where they bought their marbles and tops and Jew's-harps. The store had a high, sharp gable to the street, and showed its timbers through the roughcast of its wall, which was sprinkled with broken glass that glistened in the sun. After a while the building disappeared like a scene shifted at the theatre, and it was probably torn down. Then the boys found another toy store; but they considered the dealer mean; he asked very high prices, and he said, when a boy hung back from buying a thing that it was "a very superior article," and the boys had that for a by-word, and they holloed it at the storekeeper's boy when they wanted to plague him. There were two bakeries, and at the American bakery there were small sponge-cakes, which were the nicest cakes in the world, for a cent apiece; at the Dutch bakery there were pretzels, with salt and ashes sticking on them, that the Dutch boys liked; but the American boys made fun of them, and the bread at the Dutch bakery was always sour. There were four or five taverns where drink was always sold and drunkards often to be seen; and there was one Dutch tavern, but the Dutchmen generally went to the brewery for their beer, and drank it there. The boys went to the brewery, to get yeast for their mothers; and they liked to linger among the great heaps of malt, and the huge vats wreathed in steam, and sending out a pleasant smell. The floors were always wet, and the fat, pale Dutchmen, working about in the vapory air, never spoke to the boys, who were afraid of them. They took a boy's bottle and filled it with foaming yeast, and then took his cent, all in a silence so oppressive that he scarcely dared to breathe. My boy wondered where they kept the boy they were bringing up to drink beer; but it would have been impossible to ask. The brewery overlooked the river, and you could see the south side of the bridge from its back windows, and that was very strange. It was just like the picture of the bridge in "Howe's History of Ohio," and that made it seem like a bridge in some far-off country.

There were two fire-engines in the Boy's Town; but there seemed to be something always the matter with them, so that they would not work, if there was a fire. When there was no fire, the companies sometimes pulled them up through the town to the Basin bank, and practised with them against the roofs and fronts of the pork-houses. It was almost as good as a muster to see the firemen in their red shirts and black trousers, dragging the engine at a run, two and two together, one on each side of the rope. My boy would have liked to speak to a fireman, but he never dared; and the foreman of the Neptune, which was the larger and feebler of the engines, was a figure of such worshipful splendor in his eyes that he felt as if he could not be just a common human being. He was a storekeeper, to begin with, and he was tall and slim, and his black trousers fitted him like a glove; he had a patent-leather helmet, and a brass speaking-trumpet, and he gave all his orders through this. It did not make any difference how close he was to the men, he shouted everything through the trumpet; and when they manned the breaks and began to pump, he roared at them, "Down on her, down on her, boys!" so that you would have thought the Neptune could put out the world if it was burning up. Instead of that there was usually a feeble splutter from the nozzle, and sometimes none at all, even if the hose did not break; it was fun to see the hose break. The Neptune was a favorite with the boys, though they believed that the Tremont could squirt farther, and they had a belief in its quiet efficiency which was fostered by its reticence in public. It was small and black, but the Neptune was large, and painted of a gay color lit up with gilding that sent the blood leaping through a boy's veins. The boys knew the Neptune was out of order, but they were always expecting it would come right, and in the meantime they felt that it was an honor to the town, and they followed it as proudly back to the engine-house after one of its magnificent failures as if it had been a magnificent success. The boys were always making magnificent failures themselves, and they could feel for the Neptune.

"THE ARTIST SEEMED SATISFIED HIMSELF."

Before the Hydraulic was opened, the pork-houses were the chief public attraction to the boys, and they haunted them, with a thrilling interest in the mysteries of pork-packing which none of their sensibilities revolted from. Afterwards, the cotton-mills, which were rather small brick factories, though they looked so large to the boys, eclipsed the pork-house in their regard. They were all wild to work in the mills at first, and they thought it a hardship that their fathers would not let them leave school and do it. Some few of the fellows that my boy knew did get to work in the mills; and one of them got part of his finger taken off in the machinery; it was thought a distinction among the boys, and something like having been in war. My boy's brother was so crazy to try mill-life that he was allowed to do so for a few weeks; but a few weeks were enough of it, and pretty soon the feeling about the mills all quieted down, and the boys contented themselves with their flumes and their wheel-pits, and the head-gates that let the water in on the wheels; sometimes you could find fish under the wheels when the mills were not running. The mill-doors all had "No Admittance" painted on them; and the mere sight of the forbidding words would have been enough to keep my boy away, for he had a great awe of any sort of authority; but once he went into the mill to see his brother; and another time he and some other boys got into an empty mill, where they found a painter on an upper floor painting a panorama of "Paradise Lost." This masterpiece must have been several hundred feet long; the boys disputed whether it would reach to the sawmill they could see from the windows if it was stretched out; and my boy was surprised by the effects which the painter got out of some strips of tinsel which he was attaching to the scenery of the lake of fire and brimstone at different points. The artist seemed satisfied himself with this simple means of suggesting the gleam of infernal fires. He walked off to a distance to get it in perspective, and the boys ventured so close to the paints which he had standing about by the bucketful that it seemed as if he must surely hollo at them. But he did not say anything or seem to remember that they were there. They formed such a favorable opinion of him and his art that they decided to have a panorama; but it never came to anything. In the first place they could not get the paints, let alone the muslin.

Besides the bridge, the school-houses, the court-house and jail, the port-houses and the mills, there was only one other public edifice in their town that concerned the boys, or that they could use in accomplishing the objects of their life, and this was the hall that was built while my boy could remember its rise, for public amusements. It was in this hall that he first saw a play, and then saw so many plays, for he went to the theatre every night; but for a long time it seemed to be devoted to the purposes of mesmerism. A professor highly skilled in that science, which has reappeared in these days under the name of hypnotism, made a sojourn of some weeks in the town, and besides teaching it to classes of learners who wished to practise it, gave nightly displays of its wonders. He mesmerized numbers of the boys, and made them do or think whatever he said. He would give a boy a cane, and then tell him it was a snake, and the boy would throw it away like lightning. He would get a lot of boys, and mount them on chairs, and then tell them that they were at a horse-race, and the boys would gallop astride of their chairs round and round till he stopped them. Sometimes he would scare them almost to death, with a thunder-storm that he said was coming on; at other times he would make them go in swimming, on the dusty floor, and they would swim all over it in their best clothes, and would think they were in the river.

There were some people who did not believe in the professor, or the boys either. One of these people was an officer of the army who was staying a while in the Boy's Town, and perhaps had something to do with recruiting troops for the Mexican War. He came to the lecture one night, and remained with others who lingered after it was over to speak with the professor. My boy was there with his father, and it seemed to him that the officer smiled mockingly at the professor; angry words passed, and then the officer struck out at the professor. In an instant the professor put up both his fists; they flashed towards the officer's forehead, and the officer tumbled backwards. The boy could hardly believe it had happened. It seemed unreal, and of the dreamlike quality that so many facts in a child's bewildered life are of.

There were very few places of amusement or entertainment in the Boy's Town that were within a boy's reach. There were at least a dozen places where a man could get whiskey, but only one where he could get ice-cream, and the boys were mostly too poor and too shy to visit this resort. But there used to be a pleasure-garden on the outskirts of the town, which my boy remembered visiting when he was a very little fellow, with his brother. There were two large old mulberry-trees in this garden, and one bore white mulberries and the other black mulberries, and when you had paid your fip to come in, you could eat all the mulberries you wanted, for nothing. There was a tame crow that my boy understood could talk if it liked; but it only ran after him, and tried to bite his legs. Besides this attraction, there was a labyrinth, or puzzle, as the boys called it, of paths that wound in and out among bushes, so that when you got inside you were lucky if you could find your way out. My boy, though he had hold of his brother's hand, did not expect to get out; he expected to perish in that labyrinth, and he had some notion that his end would be hastened by the tame crow. His first visit to the pleasure-garden was his last; and it passed so wholly out of his consciousness that he never knew what became of it any more than if it had been taken up into the clouds.

He tasted ice-cream there for the first time, and had his doubts about it, though a sherry-glass full of it cost a fip, and it ought to have been good for such a sum as that. Later in life, he sometimes went to the saloon where it was sold in the town, and bashfully gasped out a demand for a glass, and ate it in some sort of chilly back-parlor. But the boys in that town, if they cared for such luxuries, did not miss them much, and their lives were full of such vivid interests arising from the woods and waters all about them that they did not need public amusements other than those which chance and custom afforded them. I have tried to give some notion of the pleasure they got out of the daily arrival of the packet in the Canal Basin; and it would be very unjust if I failed to celebrate the omnibus which was put on in place of the old-fashioned stage-coaches between the Boy's Town and Cincinnati. I dare say it was of the size of the ordinary city omnibus, but it looked as large to the boys then as a Pullman car would look to a boy now; and they assembled for its arrivals and departures with a thrill of civic pride such as hardly any other fact of the place could impart.

My boy remembered coming from Cincinnati in the stage when he was so young that it must have been when he first came to the Boy's Town. The distance was twenty miles, and the stage made it in four hours. It was this furious speed which gave the child his earliest illusion of trees and fences racing by while the stage seemed to stand still. Several times after that he made the journey with his father, seeming to have been gone a long age before he got back, and always so homesick that he never had any appetite at the tavern where the stage stopped for dinner midway. When it started back, he thought it would never get off the city pave and out from between its lines of houses into the free country. The boys always called Cincinnati "The City." They supposed it was the only city in the world.

"MY BOY REMEMBERS COMING FROM CINCINNATI IN THE STAGE."

Of course there was a whole state of things in the Boy's Town that the boys never knew of, or only knew by mistaken rumors and distorted glimpses. They had little idea of its politics, or commerce, or religion that was not wrong, and they only concerned themselves with persons and places so far as they expected to make use of them. But as they could make very little use of grown persons or public places, they kept away from them, and the Boy's Town was, for the most part, an affair of water-courses, and fields and woods, and the streets before the houses, and the alleys behind them.

Nearly all the houses had vegetable gardens, and some of them had flower-gardens that appeared princelier pleasaunces to my boy than he has ever seen since in Europe or America. Very likely they were not so vast or so splendid as they looked to him then; but one of them at least had beds of tulips and nasturtiums, and borders of flags and pinks, with clumps of tiger-lilies and hollyhocks; and in the grassy yard beside it there were high bushes full of snow-balls, and rose-trees with moss-roses on them. In this superb domain there were two summer-houses and a shed where bee-hives stood; at the end of the garden was a bath-house, and you could have a shower-bath, if you were of a mind to bring the water for it from the pump in the barn-yard. But this was all on a scale of unequalled magnificence; and most of the houses, which were mostly of wood, just had a good big yard with plum-trees and cherry-trees in it; and a vegetable garden at one side that the boy hated to weed. My boy's grandfather had a large and beautiful garden, with long arbors of grapes in it, that the old gentleman trimmed and cared for himself. They were delicious grapes; and there were black currants, which the grandfather liked, because he had liked them when he was a boy himself in the old country, but which no Boy's Town boy could have been induced to take as a gracious gift. Another boy had a father that had a green-house; he was a boy that would let you pull pie-plant in the garden, and would bring out sugar to let you eat it with in the green-house. His cleverness was rewarded when his father was elected governor of the state; and what made it so splendid was that his father was a Whig.

Every house, whether it had a flower-garden or not, had a woodshed, which was the place where a boy mostly received his friends, and made his kites and wagons, and laid his plots and plans for all the failures of his life. The other boys waited in the woodshed when he went in to ask his mother whether he might do this or that, or go somewhere. A boy always wanted to have a stove in the woodshed and fit it up for himself, but his mother would not let him, because he would have been certain to set the house on fire.

Each fellow knew the inside of his own house tolerably well, but seldom the inside of another fellow's house, and he knew the back-yard better than the front-yard. If he entered the house of a friend at all, it was to wait for him by the kitchen-door, or to get up to the garret with him by the kitchen-stairs. If he sometimes, and by some rare mischance, found himself in the living-rooms, or the parlor, he was very unhappy, and anxious to get out. Yet those interiors were not of an oppressive grandeur, and one was much like another. The parlor had what was called a flowered-carpet or gay pattern of ingrain on its floor, and the other rooms had rag-carpets, woven by some woman who had a loom for the work, and dyed at home with such native tints as butternut and foreign colors as logwood. The rooms were all heated with fireplaces, where wood was burned, and coal was never seen. They were lit at night with tallow-candles, which were mostly made by the housewife herself, or by lard-oil glass lamps. In the winter the oil would get so stiff with the cold that it had to be thawed out at the fire before the lamp would burn. There was no such thing as a hot-air furnace known; and the fire on the hearth was kept over from day to day all winter long, by covering a log at night with ashes; in the morning it would be a bed of coals. There were no fires in bedrooms, or at least not in a boy's bedroom, and sometimes he had to break the ice in his pitcher before he could wash; it did not take him very long to dress.

I have said that they burned wood for heating in the Boy's Town; but my boy could remember one winter when they burned ears of corn in the printing-office stove because it was cheaper. I believe they still sometimes burn corn in the West, when they are too far from a market to sell it at a paying price; but it always seems a sin and a shame that in a state pretending to be civilized food should ever be destroyed when so many are hungry. When one hears of such things one would almost think that boys could make a better state than this of the men.

XX.
TRAITS AND CHARACTERS.

In the Boy's Town a great many men gave nearly their whole time to the affairs of the state, and did hardly anything but talk politics all day; they even sat up late at night to do it. Among these politicians the Whigs were sacred in my boy's eyes, but the Democrats appeared like enemies of the human race; and one of the strangest things that ever happened to him was to find his father associating with men who came out of the Democratic party at the time he left the Whig party, and joining with them in a common cause against both. But when he understood what a good cause it was, and came to sing songs against slavery, he was reconciled, though he still regarded the Whig politicians as chief among the great ones, if not the good ones, of the earth. When he passed one of them on the street, he held his breath for awe till he got by, which was not always so very soon, for sometimes a Whig statesman wanted the whole sidewalk to himself, and it was hard to get by him. There were other people in that town who wanted the whole sidewalk, and these were the professional drunkards, whom the boys regarded as the keystones, if not corner-stones, of the social edifice. There were three or four of them, and the boys held them all, rich and poor alike, in a deep interest, if not respect, as persons of peculiar distinction. I do not think any boy realized the tragedy of those hopeless, wasted, slavish lives. The boys followed the wretched creatures, at a safe distance, and plagued them, and ran whenever one of them turned and threatened them. That was because the boys had not the experience to enable them to think rightly, or to think at all about such things, or to know what images of perdition they had before their eyes; and when they followed them and teased them, they did not know they were joining like fiends in the torment of lost souls. Some of the town-drunkards were the outcasts of good homes, which they had desolated, and some had merely destroyed in themselves that hope of any home which is the light of heaven in every human heart; but from time to time a good man held out a helping hand to one of them, and gave him the shelter of his roof, and tried to reclaim him. Then the boys saw him going about the streets, pale and tremulous, in a second-hand suit of his benefactor's clothes, and fighting hard against the tempter that beset him on every side in that town; and then some day they saw him dead drunk in a fence corner; and they did not understand how seven devils worse than the first had entered in the place which had been swept and garnished for them.

Besides the town-drunkards there were other persons in whom the boys were interested, like the two or three dandies, whom their splendor in dress had given a public importance in a community of carelessly dressed men. Then there were certain genteel loafers, young men of good families, who hung about the principal hotel, and whom the boys believed to be fighters of singular prowess. Far below these in the social scale, the boys had yet other heroes, such as the Dumb Negro and his family. Between these and the white people, among whom the boys knew of no distinctions, they were aware that there was an impassable gulf; and it would not be easy to give a notion of just the sort of consideration in which they held them. But they held the Dumb Negro himself in almost superstitious regard as one who, though a deaf-mute, knew everything that was going on, and could make you understand anything he wished. He was, in fact, a master of most eloquent pantomime; he had gestures that could not be mistaken, and he had a graphic dumb-show for persons and occupations and experiences that was delightfully vivid. For a dentist, he gave an upward twist of the hand from his jaw, and uttered a howl which left no doubt that he meant tooth-pulling; and for what would happen to a boy if he kept on misbehaving, he crossed his fingers before his face and looked through them in a way that brought the jail-window clearly before the eyes of the offender.

The boys knew vaguely that his family helped runaway slaves on their way North, and in a community that was for the most part bitterly pro-slavery these negroes were held in a sort of respect for their courageous fidelity to their race. The men were swarthy, handsome fellows, not much darker than Spaniards, and they were so little afraid of the chances which were often such fatal mischances to colored people in that day that one of them travelled through the South, and passed himself in very good company as a Cherokee Indian of rank and education.

As far as the boys knew, the civic affairs of the place were transacted entirely by two constables. Of mayors and magistrates, such as there must have been, they knew nothing, and they had not the least notion what the Whigs whom they were always trying to elect were to do when they got into office. They knew that the constables were both Democrats, but, if they thought at all about the fact, they thought their Democracy the natural outcome of their dark constabulary nature, and by no means imagined that they were constables because they were Democrats. The worse of the two, or the more merciless, was also the town-crier, whose office is now not anywhere known in America, I believe; though I heard a town-crier in a Swiss village not many years ago. In the Boy's Town the crier carried a good-sized bell; when he started out he rang it till he reached the street corner, and then he stopped, and began some such proclamation as, "O, yes! O, yes! O, yes! There will be an auction this evening at early candle-light, at Brown & Robinson's store! Dry goods, boots and shoes, hats and caps, hardware, queen's ware, and so forth, and so forth. Richard Roe, Auctioneer! Come one, come all, come everybody!" Then the crier rang his bell, and went on to the next corner, where he repeated his proclamation. After a while, the constable got a deputy to whom he made over his business of town-crier. This deputy was no other than that reckless boy who used to run out from the printing-office and shoot the turtle-doves; and he decorated his proclamation with quips and quirks of his own invention, and with personal allusions to his employer, who was auctioneer as well as constable. But though he was hail-fellow with every boy in town, and although every boy rejoiced in his impudence, he was so panoplied in the awfulness of his relation to the constabulary functions that, however remote it was, no boy would have thought of trifling with him when he was on duty. If ever a boy holloed something at him when he was out with his crier's bell, he turned and ran as hard as he could, and as if from the constable himself.

The boys knew just one other official, and that was the gauger, whom they watched at a respectful distance, when they found him employed with his mysterious instruments gauging the whiskey in the long rows of barrels on the Basin bank. They did not know what the process was, and I own that I do not know to this day what it was. My boy watched him with the rest, and once he ventured upon a bold and reckless act. He had so long heard that it was whiskey which made people drunk that at last the notion came to have an irresistible fascination for him, and he determined to risk everything, even life itself, to know what whiskey was like. As soon as the gauger had left them, he ran up to one of the barrels where he had seen a few drops fall from his instrument when he lifted it from the bunghole, and plunged the tip of his little finger into the whiskey, and then put it to his tongue. He expected to become drunk instantly, if not to end a town-drunkard there on the spot; but the whiskey only tasted very disgusting; and he was able to get home without help. Still, I would not advise any other boy to run the risk he took in this desperate experiment.

There was a time not long after that when he really did get drunk, but it was not with whiskey. One morning after a rain, when the boys were having fun in one of those open canal-boats with the loose planks which the over-night shower had set afloat, a fellow came up and said he had got some tobacco that was the best kind to learn to chew with. Every boy who expected to be anything in the world expected to chew tobacco; for all the packet-drivers chewed; and it seemed to my boy that his father and grandfather and uncles were about the only people who did not chew. If they had only smoked, it would have been something, but they did not even smoke; and the boy felt that he had a long arrears of manliness to bring up, and that he should have to retrieve his family in spite of itself from the shame of not using tobacco in any form. He knew that his father abhorred it, but he had never been explicitly forbidden to smoke or chew, for his father seldom forbade him anything explicitly, and he gave himself such freedom of choice in the matter that when the boy with the tobacco began to offer it around, he judged it right to take a chew with the rest. The boy said it was a peculiar kind of tobacco, and was known as molasses-tobacco because it was so sweet. The other boys did not ask how he came to know its name, or where he got it; boys never ask anything that it would be well for them to know; but they accepted his theory, and his further statement that it was of a mildness singularly adapted to learners, without misgiving. The boy was himself chewing vigorously on a large quid, and launching the juice from his lips right and left like a grown person; and my boy took as large a bite as his benefactor bade him. He found it as sweet as he had been told it was, and he acknowledged the aptness of its name of molasses-tobacco; it seemed to him a golden opportunity to acquire a noble habit on easy terms. He let the quid rest in his cheek as he had seen men do, when he was not crushing it between his teeth, and for some moments he poled his plank up and down the canal-boat with a sense of triumph that nothing marred. Then, all of a sudden, he began to feel pale. The boat seemed to be going round, and the sky wheeling overhead; the sun was dodging about very strangely. Drops of sweat burst from the boy's forehead; he let fall his pole, and said that he thought he would go home. The fellow who gave him the tobacco began to laugh, and the other fellows to mock, but my boy did not mind them. Somehow, he did not know how, he got out of the canal-boat and started homeward; but at every step the ground rose as high as his knees before him, and then when he got his foot high enough, and began to put it down, the ground was not there. He was deathly sick, as he reeled and staggered on, and when he reached home, and showed himself white and haggard to his frightened mother, he had scarcely strength to gasp out a confession of his attempt to retrieve the family honor by learning to chew tobacco. In another moment nature came to his relief, and then he fell into a deep sleep which lasted the whole afternoon, so that it seemed to him the next day when he woke up, glad to find himself alive, if not so very lively. Perhaps he had swallowed some of the poisonous juice of the tobacco; perhaps it had acted upon his brain without that. His father made no very close inquiry into the facts, and he did not forbid him the use of tobacco. It was not necessary; in that one little experiment he had got enough for a whole lifetime. It shows that, after all, a boy is not so hard to satisfy in everything.

There were some people who believed that tobacco would keep off the fever-and-ague, which was so common then in that country, or at any rate that it was good for the toothache. In spite of the tobacco, there were few houses where ague was not a familiar guest, however unwelcome. If the family was large, there was usually a chill every day; one had it one day, and another the next, so that there was no lapse. This was the case in my boy's family, after they moved to the Faulkner house, which was near the Basin and its water-soaked banks; but they accepted the ague as something quite in the course of nature, and duly broke it up with quinine. Some of the boys had chills at school; and sometimes, after they had been in swimming, they would wait round on the bank till a fellow had his chill out, and then they would all go off together and forget about it. The next day that fellow would be as well as any one; the third day his chill would come on again, but he did not allow it to interfere with his business or pleasure, and after a while the ague would seem to get tired of it, and give up altogether. That strange earth-spirit who was my boy's friend simply beat the ague, as it were, on its own ground. He preferred a sunny spot to have his chill in, a cosy fence-corner or a warm back door-step, or the like; but as for the fever that followed the chill, he took no account of it whatever, or at least made no provision for it.

The miasm which must have filled the air of the place from so many natural and artificial bodies of fresh water showed itself in low fevers, which were not so common as ague, but common enough. The only long sickness that my boy could remember was intermittent fever, which seemed to last many weeks, and which was a kind of bewilderment rather than a torment. When it was beginning he appeared to glide down the stairs at school without touching the steps with his feet, and afterwards his chief trouble was in not knowing, when he slept, whether he had really been asleep or not. But there was rich compensation for this mild suffering in the affectionate petting which a sick boy always gets from his mother when his malady takes him from his rough little world and gives him back helpless to her tender arms again. Then she makes everything in the house yield to him; none of the others are allowed to tease him or cross him in the slightest thing. They have to walk lightly; and when he is going to sleep, if they come into the room, they have got to speak in a whisper. She sits by his bed and fans him; she smooths the pillow and turns its cool side up under his hot and aching head; she cooks dainty dishes to tempt his sick appetite, and brings them to him herself. She is so good and kind and loving that he cannot help having some sense of it all, and feeling how much better she is than anything on earth. His little ruffian world drifts far away from him. He hears the yells and shouts of the boys in the street without a pang of envy or longing; in his weakness, his helplessness, he becomes a gentle and innocent child again; and heaven descends to him out of his mother's heart.

XXI.
LAST DAYS.

I have already told that my boy's father would not support General Taylor, the Whig candidate for President, because he believed him, as the hero of a pro-slavery war, to be a friend of slavery. At this time he had a large family of little children, and he had got nothing beyond a comfortable living from the newspaper which he had published for eight years; if he must give that up, he must begin life anew heavily burdened. Perhaps he thought it need not come to his giving up his paper, that somehow affairs might change. But his newspaper would have gone to nothing in his hands if he had tried to publish it as a Free Soil paper after the election of the Whig candidate; so he sold it, and began to cast about for some other business; how anxiously, my boy was too young to know. He only felt the relief that the whole family felt for a while at getting out of the printing business; the boys wanted to go into almost anything else: the drug-business, or farming, or a paper-mill, or anything. The elder brother knew all the anxiety of the time, and shared it fully with the mother, whose acquiescence in what the father thought right was more than patient; she abode courageously in the suspense, the uncertainty of the time; and she hoped for something from the father's endeavors in the different ways he turned. At one time there was much talk in the family of using the fibre of a common weed in making paper, which he thought he could introduce; perhaps it was the milk-weed; but he could not manage it, somehow; and after a year of inaction he decided to go into another newspaper. By this time the boys had made their peace with the printing business, and the father had made his with the Whig party. He had done what it must have been harder to do than to stand out against it; he had publicly owned that he was mistaken in regard to

Taylor, who had not become the tool of the slaveholders, but had obeyed the highest instincts of the party and served the interests of freedom, though he was himself a slaveholder and the hero of an unjust war.

It was then too late, however, for the father to have got back his old newspaper, even if he had wished, and the children heard, with the elation that novelty brings to all children, old or young, that they were going away from the Boy's Town, to live in another place. It was a much larger place and was even considered a city, though it was not comparable to Cincinnati, so long the only known city in the world.

My boy was twelve years old by that time, and was already a swift compositor, though he was still so small that he had to stand on a chair to reach the case in setting type on Taylor's inaugural message. But what he lacked in stature he made up in gravity of demeanor; and he got the name of "The Old Man" from the printers as soon as he began to come about the office, which he did almost as soon as he could walk. His first attempt in literature, an essay on the vain and disappointing nature of human life, he set up and printed off himself in his sixth or seventh year; and the printing-office was in some sort his home, as well as his school, his university. He could no more remember learning to set type than he could remember learning to read; and in after-life he could not come within smell of the ink, the dusty types, the humid paper, of a printing-office without that tender swelling of the heart which so fondly responds to any memory-bearing perfume: his youth, his boyhood, almost his infancy came back to him in it. He now looked forward eagerly to helping on the new paper, and somewhat proudly to living in the larger place the family were going to. The moment it was decided he began to tell the boys that he was going to live in a city, and he felt that it gave him distinction. He had nothing but joy in it, and he did not dream that as the time drew near it could be sorrow. But when it came at last, and he was to leave the house, the town, the boys, he found himself deathly homesick. The parting days were days of gloom; the parting was an anguish of bitter tears. Nothing consoled him but the fact that they were going all the way to the new place in a canal-boat, which his father chartered for the trip. My boy and his brother had once gone to Cincinnati in a canal-boat, with a friendly captain of their acquaintance, and, though they were both put to sleep in a berth so narrow that when they turned they fell out on the floor, the glory of the adventure remained with him, and he could have thought of nothing more delightful than such another voyage. The household goods were piled up in the middle of the boat, and the family had a cabin forward, which seemed immense to the children. They played in it and ran races up and down the long canal-boat roof, where their father and mother sometimes put their chairs and sat to admire the scenery.

As my boy could remember very few incidents of this voyage afterwards, I dare say he spent a great part of it with his face in a book, and was aware of the landscape only from time to time when he lifted his eyes from the story he was reading. That was apt to be the way with him; and before he left the Boy's Town the world within claimed him more and more. He ceased to be that eager comrade he had once been; sometimes he left his book with a sigh; and he saw much of the outer world through a veil of fancies quivering like an autumn haze between him and its realities, softening their harsh outlines, and giving them a fairy coloring. I think he would sometimes have been better employed in looking directly at them; but he had to live his own life, and I cannot live it over for him. The season was the one of all others best fitted to win him to the earth, and in a measure it did. It was spring, and along the tow-path strutted the large, glossy blackbirds which had just come back, and made the boys sick with longing to kill them, they offered such good shots. But the boys had no powder with them, and at any rate the captain would not have stopped his boat, which was rushing on at the rate of two miles an hour, to let them pick up a bird, if they had hit it. They were sufficiently provisioned without the game, however; the mother had baked bread, and boiled a ham, and provided sugar-cakes in recognition of the holiday character of the voyage, and they had the use of the boat cooking-stove for their tea and coffee. The boys had to content themselves with such sense of adventure as they could get out of going ashore when the boat was passing through the locks, or staying aboard and seeing the water burst and plunge in around the boat. They had often watched this thrilling sight at the First Lock, but it had a novel interest now. As their boat approached the lock, the lower gates were pushed open by men who set their breasts to the long sweeps or handles of the gates, and when the boat was fairly inside of the stone-walled lock they were closed behind her. Then the upper gates, which opened against the dull current, and were kept shut by its pressure, were opened a little, and the waters rushed and roared into the lock, and began to lift the boat. The gates were opened wider and wider, till the waters poured a heavy cataract into the lock, where the boat tossed on their increasing volume, and at last calmed themselves to the level within. Then the boat passed out through the upper gates, on even water, and the voyage to the next lock began. At first it was rather awful, and the little children were always afraid when they came to a lock, but the boys enjoyed it after the first time. They would have liked to take turns driving the pair of horses that drew the boat, but it seemed too bold a wish, and I think they never proposed it; they did not ask, either, to relieve the man at the helm.

They arrived safely at their journey's end, without any sort of accident. They had made the whole forty miles in less than two days, and were all as well as when they started, without having suffered for a moment from seasickness. The boat drew up at the towpath just before the stable belonging to the house which the father had already taken, and the whole family at once began helping the crew put the things ashore. The boys thought it would have been a splendid stable to keep the pony in, only they had sold the pony; but they saw in an instant that it would do for a circus as soon as they could get acquainted with enough boys to have one.

The strangeness of the house and street, and the necessity of meeting the boys of the neighborhood, and paying with his person for his standing among them, kept my boy interested for a time, and he did not realize at first how much he missed the Boy's Town and all the familiar fellowships there, and all the manifold privileges of the place. Then he began to be very homesick, and to be torn with the torment of a divided love. His mother, whom he loved so dearly, so tenderly, was here, and wherever she was, that was home; and yet home was yonder, far off, at the end of those forty inexorable miles, where he had left his life-long mates. The first months there was a dumb heartache at the bottom of every pleasure and excitement. There were many excitements, not the least of which was the excitement of helping get out a tri-weekly and then a daily newspaper, instead of the weekly that his father had published in the Boy's Town. Then that dear friend of his brother and himself, the apprentice who knew all about "Monte Cristo," came to work with them and live with them again, and that was a great deal; but he did not bring the Boy's Town with him; and when they each began to write a new historical romance, the thought of the beloved scenes amidst which they had planned their first was a pang that nothing could assuage. During the summer the cholera came; the milkman, though naturally a cheerful person, said that the people around where he lived were dying off like flies; and the funerals, three and four, five and six, ten and twelve a day, passed before the door; and all the brooding horror of the pestilence sank deep into the boy's morbid soul. Then he fell sick of the cholera himself; and, though it was a mild attack, he lay in the Valley of the Shadow of Death while it lasted, and waited the worst with such terror that when he kept asking her if he should get well, his mother tried to reason with him, and to coax him out of his fear. Was he afraid to die, she asked him, when he knew that heaven was so much better, and he would be in the care of such love as never could come to him on earth? He could only gasp back that he *was* afraid to die; and she could only turn from reconciling him with the other world to assuring him that he was in no danger of leaving this.

I sometimes think that if parents would deal rightly and truly with children about death from the beginning, some of the fear of it might be taken away. It seems to me that it is partly because death is hushed up and ignored between them that it rests such a burden on the soul; but if children were told as soon as they are old enough that death is a part of nature, and not a calamitous accident, they would be somewhat strengthened to meet it. My boy had been taught that this world was only an illusion, a shadow thrown from the real world beyond; and no doubt his father and mother believed what they taught him; but he had always seen them anxious to keep the illusion, and in his turn he clung to the vain shadow with all the force of his being.

He got well of the cholera, but not of the homesickness, and after a while he was allowed to revisit the Boy's Town. It could only have been three or four months after he had left it, but it already seemed a very long time; and he figured himself returning as stage-heroes do to the scenes of their childhood, after an absence of some fifteen years. He fancied that if the boys did not find him grown, they would find him somehow changed, and that he would dazzle them with the light accumulated by his residence in a city. He was going to stay with his grandmother, and he planned to make a long stay; for he was very fond of her, and he liked the quiet and comfort of her pleasant house. He must have gone back by the canal-packet, but his memory kept no record of the fact, and afterwards he knew only of having arrived, and of searching about in a ghostly fashion for his old comrades. They may have been at school; at any rate he found very few of them; and with them he was certainly strange enough; too strange, even. They received him with a kind of surprise; and they could not begin playing together at once in the old way. He went to all the places that were so dear to him; but he felt in them the same kind of refusal, or reluctance, that he felt in the boys. His heart began to ache again, he did not quite know why; only it ached. When he went up from his grandmother's to look at the Faulkner house, he realized that it was no longer home, and he could not bear the sight of it. There were other people living in it; strange voices sounded from the open doors, strange faces peered from the windows.

He came back to his grandmother's, bruised and defeated, and spent the morning indoors reading. After dinner he went out again, and hunted up that queer earth-spirit who had been so long and closely his only friend. He at least was not changed; he was as unwashed and as unkempt as ever; but he seemed shy of my poor boy. He had probably never been shaken hands with in his life before; he dropped my boy's hand; and they stood looking at each other, not knowing what to say. My boy had on his best clothes, which he wore so as to affect the Boy's Town boys with the full splendor of a city boy. After all, he was not so very splendid, but his presence altogether was too much for the earth-spirit, and he vanished out of his consciousness like an apparition.

After school was out in the afternoon, he met more of the boys, but none of them knew just what to do with him. The place that he had once had in their lives was filled; he was an outsider, who might be suffered among them, but he was no longer of them. He did not understand this at once, nor well know what hurt him. But something was gone that could not be called back, something lost that could not be found.

At tea-time his grandfather came home and gravely made him welcome; the uncle who was staying with them was jovially kind. But a heavy homesickness weighed down the child's heart, which now turned from the Boy's Town as longingly as it had turned towards it before.

They all knelt down with the grandfather before they went to the table. There had been a good many deaths from cholera during the day, and the grandfather prayed for grace and help amidst the pestilence that walketh in darkness and wasteth at noonday in such a way that the boy felt there would be very little of either for him unless he got home at once. All through the meal that followed he was trying to find the courage to say that he must go home. When he managed to say it, his grandmother and aunt tried to comfort and coax him, and his uncle tried to shame him, out of his homesickness, to joke it off, to make him laugh. But his grandfather's tender heart was moved. He could not endure the child's mute misery; he said he must go home if he wished.

In half an hour the boy was on the canal-packet speeding homeward at the highest pace of the three-horse team, and the Boy's Town was out of sight. He could not sleep for excitement that night, and he came and spent the time talking on quite equal terms with the steersman, one of the canalers whom he had admired afar in earlier and simpler days. He found him a very amiable fellow, by no means haughty, who began to tell him funny stories, and who even let him take the helm for a while. The rudder-handle was of polished iron, very different from the clumsy wooden affair of a freight-boat; and the packet made in a single night the distance which the boy's family had been nearly two days in travelling when they moved away from the Boy's Town.

He arrived home for breakfast a travelled and experienced person, and wholly cured of that longing for his former home that had tormented him before he revisited its scenes. He now fully gave himself up to his new environment, and looked forward and not backward. I do not mean to say that he ceased to love the Boy's Town; that he could not do and never did. But he became more and more aware that the past was gone from him forever, and that he could not return to it. He did not forget it, but cherished its memories the more fondly for that reason.

There was no bitterness in it, and no harm that he could not hope would easily be forgiven him. He had often been foolish, and sometimes he had been wicked; but he had never been such a little fool or such a little sinner but he had wished for more sense and more grace. There are some great fools and great sinners who try to believe in after-life that they are the manlier men because they have been silly and mischievous boys, but he has never believed that. He is glad to have had a boyhood fully rounded out with all a boy's interests and pleasures, and he is glad that his lines were cast in the Boy's Town; but he knows, or believes he knows, that whatever is good in him now came from what was good in him then; and he is sure that the town was delightful chiefly because his home in it was happy. The town was small and the boys there were hemmed in by their inexperience and ignorance; but the simple home was large with vistas that stretched to the ends of the earth, and it was serenely bright with a father's reason and warm with a mother's love.

THE END.

Made in the USA
Lexington, KY
02 January 2016